TIME TO DIE

RICHARD GERBER

Published by

RG Livre Publisher
2021

Book cover design and formatting services by SelfPublishingLab.com

ISBN:
978-1-7372249-1-4 (pbk)
978-1-7372249-2-1 (ebk)

*For all the women, who in their teens were date raped,
by the dirtbag predators who were never identified, caught,
or punished for their dastardly, low mentality crimes.*

Based on a true crime incident—this story is a work of fiction.

All the names are fictitious to protect the innocent from embarrassment and the guilty from vigilante justice. The towns, cities, and some businesses are real, some are not. The churches are fictitious.

All addresses of the victims, heroes and predators are the inventions of the author. The predators know who they are, and where they are.

Hell is coming.

Contents

1

Elizabeth felt tortured. Her insides were churning as she sat close to the phone. Will she be saved from this misery? Why hasn't Abigail called?

It kept getting dark earlier each day as early October, 1965, slowly moved towards winter. The sun still had at least an hour before it set and Elizabeth Crenshaw was bored. It was Friday with no place to go and nothing to do but to stay out of her parent's way. Elizabeth was the oldest of four sisters at sixteen. Lizz and Della followed a year part, fifteen and fourteen. Elizabeth, Betty as she was known to her friends, did have *that* younger sister, Karen, who was eight years younger than Betty. Each of the older sisters hated the young snot—daddy's favorite. Betty would like to slap the *snot* out of the little brat—if she could. But she can't, so she'd have to put up with It. Yes, It. Her sister was an It. One day she'd make her parent's pay attention to her. *If Abigail calls soon, I might be able to get out-ta here.*

Betty was prepared. She looked good for a party. Form fitting black slacks with a pink tank top that came to the waist. On her feet were black flats. No socks, so she stood only a half inch taller than her 5'3" height. Her frosted blonde hair parted in the middle and fell to her shoulders. Her blue eyes spoke volumes more than her thin lips. A small nose graced her face.

Her father's real last name was Krauze. Her father's mother's maiden name was Sawicki. Her father, Rayder, a Polish first name that he kept, got into some kind of a fight with his family and changed his last name right at the end of World War II. Times were tough for him and his new wife, and thought the problem to be, that he was Polish. So, he took his last name and his mother's last name and combined them into Crenshaw—close enough for him.

Six months after Betty was born, she was "loaned" to her maternal grandparents. The official reason was financial hardship—so her parents said. Her mother had just become pregnant again. The father was worried over how to feed and clothe himself and three other people. The mother, Frances, had approached her parents for a loan. She ate her humble pie. Frances' father had a better idea. As a supervisor he could get Rayder Crenshaw a job at Bethlehem Steel's Sparrows Point Plant, and with his wife, he would take care of Betty. So off went baby Betty to her grandparents. Betty knew her grandparents as daddy and mommy. Sometimes her real family would visit her, which would consist of two more girls—all the girls were around a year apart. At age six her world turned upside down, she was given back to her real parents. The grandmother had died and granddaddy's new love interest didn't want Betty or any kid. She went from an only child, with her own toys, her own bedroom, in a large house, in the affluent Baltimore suburb of Bel Air, to a small apartment in Dundalk, Maryland, across the street from a distillery yet, with two other younger sisters, whom she didn't really know. She had brought her toys with her and put them in a corner of the small bedroom she shared with her two sisters.

Then her life, and the lives of the other two girls, got worse. Lizz got the worst of the three sisters. The father, more often when he drank whiskey, would beat her with a belt, fly swatter, or his hand if he couldn't find something better. Betty and Della weren't beaten as bad or as often. Betty had gumption sometimes and ran out of the house. Then Della or Lizz took the brunt. Sometimes Betty would be fondled by her father and she felt she couldn't do anything about that. She did feel that it wasn't right and tried to hide from him, especially when he drank.

Her early teen years weren't much better. Sometimes, when the parents were out doing whatever, the three young teen girls would find the hidden whiskey bottles and carefully pour some into their glasses mixing it with Coca Cola. Then they would refill the bottle with water. Daddy never noticed. If he did notice that some was missing, he blamed it on Frances.

The snot was born a few years later. Inevitably Betty was rebellious and had every reason to be. Abandonment, no affection given to her, or to any of the other sisters. Sexual abuse, as well as unjust corporal punishments were given to the older girls. They were often pushed aside in favor of the snot, Karen.

Please phone, ring. The call from Abigail was her only escape—if she called.

Everyone was watching TV, a show the older girls didn't want to watch. The Snot Princess wanted to watch "Get Smart." Betty thought it was dumb.

The phone rang and all the girls jumped up to get it. Betty grabbed it first.

"It's for me," she snapped with a happy look.

She turned her back to them and spoke low when she talked.

"Well…I don't know. I mean I'd love to but, you know, dad's home."

Betty listened to her friend, Abigail, on the other end.

"I don't know. I'll ask my mother, she's easier." She put her hand over the mouthpiece.

"Mom, Abigail wants to know if I could spend the night with her."

"No!" her father yelled.

"Oh, Rayder, quit yelling," Frances said.

"She can stay home."

"But dad, I don't get to go out hardly."

"I said…"

"Rayder, let her go. I did that when I was a teenager. She needs to get out once in a while."

Rayder opened his mouth to say something.

"Please dad. I'll do the laundry tomorrow. Please!"

"Let her go, Ray. She's sixteen. And it's over at Abigail's house. You know her."

"Yeah, but I don't know her parents."

"Oh, I'm sure they're okay." Frances tried to reassure. "If the child is good, the parents are good."

Betty chimed in, "They'll be there." Knowing that they wouldn't be.

"I wanna go too!" Karen, the brat interrupted, as always.

Gushing, Rayder said, "It's only for big girls, sweetie." He then looked at Betty. "Go ahead and spend the night. But be home early in the morning."

"I will," Betty promised. Into the phone: "My dad said yes." She listened some more and said, "Great, I'll see you soon."

"You girls are going to make my hair prematurely gray." His head still had a healthy, thick crop of black hair.

Betty walked from her house to her friend's on Detroit Avenue and was greeted by Abigail Beecher before she could knock.

"Come, come in. It's good to see you. We're gonna have fun tonight. What took you so long?"

"I was walking by Tom's house and he called to me. Said he had something to give me."

"By the smell, I think you started the party all ready."

"Yeah, and I have a buzz already. He had some sloe gin and I had two full glasses." Betty wobbled slightly before plopping into an overstuffed chair.

"That's no fair. Is Tom coming too?"

"No. Girlfriend's coming. No parents. So, you know."

"Yeah, I know," Abigail bitterly muttered. That was her old boyfriend. He had popped her cherry.

"When Jesse gets here with his good stuff I gotta catch up." Abigail scoffed. She grabbed her lit cigarette from the ashtray and took a drag.

The doorbell rang. Abigail ran to it and swung it open. "Hey, Jesse, whacha bring?"

"The good stuff, hon. No Boone's Farm or Ripple here."

Abigail grabbed the two sacks from him and hurried to the kitchen.

"I'll get three glasses."

"Gonna need more than three."

Jesse Delaney walked into the living room leaving a trail of smoke from the cigarette dangling out of the right corner of his mouth. Following him were four other boys, all under age, one sixteen, two seventeens and Jerry Gannon, who was eighteen. Twenty-year-old Jesse was almost legal but looked older, so he got away with buying the wine. A loser, Jesse dropped out of school a few years before and the "cool" kids made sure they befriended him.

Jesse's alcohol buying was made easier, since just about every corner on every block in Baltimore City stood a bar or package goods store. By law, the bars or clubs were split—one side was the liquor store and the other was the drinking bar area.

The boys looked over at Betty, slouching in the overstuffed chair. Clint, one of the seventeen-year-olds, smoke from his ciggy engulfing him, asked, "What's your name, hon."

"Betty," she giggled.

"Looks like she already started," Jerry grinned.

"Yup, and feeling no pain."

Sixteen-year-old Scott Turner said, "We got to catch up. Where's the glasses?"

"Come and get it guys. They're all full," Abigail said.

Scott grabbed two and hurried to Betty.

"Here you go, Bet."

"It's Betty, you got it, Bud?" She took a sip.

"Whoa," Jerry said. "She straightened you out."

They all laughed. Then all took large gulps, with Jerry coughing slightly. "Man, that's good stuff," he said hoarsely.

The doorbell rang again. Abigail went over and opened it. "Come in, girls. The party just started. 'Cept Betty; she's already two sheets to the wind." The three girls piled in. Two sixteen and the other seventeen. Mary Leon, 16, was another friend of Betty.

"Your dad let you come to the party?"

"Doesn't know it's a, *hic,* party. Par-doan me."

They all laughed again.

"This is gonna be a good party," Scott said.

"Can't Buy Me Love" played on the record player. Jerry and one of the girls were dancing. The others sat or stood, smoking, drinking and talking. Clint sat on the arm of Betty's chair, talking trash.

"My name's Clint but call me Flint. School's a drag. You ought-ta drop out."

"Can't. Parents won't let me," Betty slurred.

"Bummer."

"Gimme a drag," Betty ordered. Clint held the cigarette to her lips. She inhaled and blew out the excess smoke. "Let's dance."

She struggled out of the chair. Joining the other two couples. She started doing the *Bodie Green,* a popular "dirty" sexy dance that originated in Baltimore a year earlier. The guys started to cheer her on and she obliged.

Abigail had a record player that she put a long tube-like adapter on it that would hold a few 45s at a time. The next record dropped was "Shotgun".

An hour later Jesse announced that he'd be back shortly with a pack of cigarettes and another bottle. "We'll keep this party going."

Betty said, "Man this stuff is good." She put the glass to her mouth and consumed half of it.

Abigail warned her, "Slow down, Betty."

"Sure, sure," slurring her words. She didn't care about any consequences.

Scott sidled up to Clint, and whispered, "She's gonna be easy soon."

Clint licked his lips. "Yeah, and looking good too."

Scott Turner was in her grade at the High School but not in any of her classes. He heard that she was one of the nice girls but had a chip on her shoulder. He didn't want her to get to know him if they scored with her tonight. The other guys were older but he thought he was the smart one. He would have to be smart and lead these guys if they got her. He thought about future complications, if any. He kept an eye on Clint.

Another record dropped and "Satisfaction" blared from the record player.

Mary went over to Betty and bent over. "Slow down, girl. You don't want to give them no ideas."

"Oh phoo, I can handle my dinks and I can handle 'em. They ain't goin' for nothin'."

"You're sixteen. You shouldn't be drinking," Mary scolded.

"You're not my mother! Fly away!"

Mary turned walking off mumbling, *suit yourself.*

Shortly, Jesse bounded through the door carrying two bottles. "Let the party continue!"

He sat the bottles of Italian wine on the dining table.

The kids sashayed towards it and filled their glasses.

Betty made a slow awkward way back to the chair, turned around and plopped into it, spilling some of the drink. "Ah, sheets."

Clint ran his fingers through his black hair to get it back on top of his head and out of his eyes. He squinted his piecing dark eyes often. He needed his Beatle cut, cut. He moseyed toward her with his *kool walk.* "Here you go hon, take mine. It's full." He took her glass.

Smiling crookedly Betty slurred, "Wall tanks."

Clint sat on the arm of the overstuffed chair. "I seen you in school. In the halls."

"Doan member seen you." She indulged herself with another swallow.

"You look good in those pants," he commented.

"Tanks. You too I'm sure." She laughed, then giggled. "Whoa, my head's a spinnin'."

"You might need some air."

Clint rose and headed toward Jesse. "Hey Jesse, Betty needs some air. You got the car, let's go for a ride." He winked. The booze and easy prey had the predators on the move. This is why they came to the party. This is what they were hoping for. A score.

"Okay," skinny Jesse Delaney agreed and headed out the door. He was sporting a *Chicago* haircut, flat on top, long on the sides. The other guys followed, seventeen-year-old Kenneth Black, "Joe College" Scott Turner and Jerry Gannon. Turner and Gannon had some form of Beatle haircut— not Black, he still had a flat top.

"Let me help you up, Betty," Clint Zabinski said. "You need some air."

Betty wobbled up and said, "Whoa."

Scott confirmed, "Yeah, you *need* air."

"Yew betcha," she replied. "I can walk myself," as Scott held her arm.

"Okay. Let's go."

Abigail rushed over to her. "Don't go Betty. You're drunk."

The other girls came over to her. "Don't go Betty," two girls said. Another said, "It's not safe."

"I'm going. I need air." She smiled drunkenly, eyes half open, right lid drooping slightly.

She left teetering, with Clint holding and guiding her into the backseat of a Super Sport. Clint backed away and Scott followed her in. Jerry got into the backseat from the other side. Jesse jumped behind the wheel into the driver's seat of his 1962 red Chevy SS. Clint rode shotgun and pulled the door shut.

"Hey, what about me?' Kenny Black asked.

"No room, Kenny. Sorry", Jesse said.

Smiling up at him, Clint said, "Maybe next time, Kenny. Get rid of the flat top, square."

The girls ran up to the car and begged Betty to stay with them.

"We're goin' for a ride." Betty slurred, her head resting on the seat back.

The guys all said in unison, "Right."

Jesse fired the engine and peeled out.

The girls just stood looking. Abigail had tears in her eyes. "Maybe I should call the police", Betty's best friend said.

"No, she'll get in trouble with her parents."

Lexi said, "She'll be alright. I think they're okay guys."

Another girl asserted, "No guy is nice when a girl is soused." She finished her drink. "How about another?"

"Go get it, but I don't like *this*," Abigail cried as she ran back into the house. The other girls staggered after her.

Kenny followed them in. "Hey, you guys still have me." No one paid attention to him.

Mary Slurred. "Let's fill our glasses and wait for them to come back."

"Good idea," Kenny said.

"Twist and Shout" started to play.

"Who wants to dance?" Kenny asked. No one answered. "Abigail, your party isn't where it's at. I'm leaving."

"Bye Kenny pooh," Lexi taunted.

"Screw you," Kenny said as he charged out the door, slamming it.

Abigail ran to her bedroom and laid across her bed crying. After a few minutes she sniffled her way to the phone and dialed a friend. She started sobbing.

"Freddy, it's Abby, some guys took Betty in their car and she's drunk out of her mind and they're going to do something to her I know, can you get on your motorcycle and find them? They just left…"

"Whoa, slow down Abby, stop crying and give me some details." Sobbing, "Okay." After a minute she got control of herself and told him everything—between whimpers.

2

"Hey, you wanna see the submarine races?" Clint asked.

"Shut up, Flint," scolded Jesse.

"Where to?" Scott asked.

"Saint Helena's Park should be good."

"What time is it?" Jerry asked.

"Late night or early morning," Clint said.

They all laughed and Betty droned, "You're funny."

Jesse drove slowly to keep the car from rumbling a loud chorus approaching the park. On Woodley Road, the rowhouses were across the street from the entrance. No lights on at the park's small parking area. He drove into the parking area to get a closer look. A small clubhouse stood a short distance away. No other lovers were around. Jesse studied the area for a few seconds. He thought it didn't feel right tonight.

Turning the car around, Jesse pulled out and he drove through the low-income area of St. Helena, came to a short dog leg road and made a right onto Broening Highway. There were a couple of other spots for "submarines races", but they were farther away.

"Oh boy, we're going to the races," Clint said.

Fuming Jesse said in a strangled voice. "Shut the hell up, dope."

Slurring, with her head lolling Betty said, "Races."

Guiding the car off Broening Highway, Jesse said, "I think here's the best parking spot around. City cops hardly ever come through." Turning the headlights off and using only the parking lights he parked the car as close to the railroad tracks as possible. Then he killed the lights. Across the highway was the Maryland Port Administration's Dundalk Marine Terminal and its buildings. The fenced in parking lot was closer to them than the buildings. The main building stood a thousand yards south or to the east of the car lot for employees. Few cars were in the lot.

Jesse knew where the boundary line was between the county and the city. He had parked on the city side, just before the Colgate Creek Bridge. The strip of dirt area that they had parked was about three fourths of a mile long, inclusive of city and county. It was popular with the make out artists, of which there weren't many of them tonight. The courtesy the kids gave each other meant they tried to stay as far away from each other as they could.

As Jesse turned off the engine he heard, "Get off uv me." Betty was laying across the back seat. Jerry held her left arm while Scott unzipped her slacks and struggled to get them off. Scott had already pulled her shoes off. Since Jerry was by her head, he now held both her arms as she started to struggle. He had to assert more muscle effort to keep her arms from moving. Clint smiled as he watched and waited. Jesse looked ahead and smoked.

Slurring in a low voice Betty said, "Get off." After that she stopped fighting and laid there as Jerry held her arms and Scott entered her. After he finished, they quickly switched places and Jerry had his way with her.

Clint climbed over the seat pushing Jerry out of the way, who had to exit the car. Scott grabbed her top and lifted it over her breasts, then pulled up her bra. He quickly sucked her left breast.

Her drooping eyes were open. She saw their faces and tried to block everything out. She couldn't really feel anything but knew what they were doing. A classic gang bang with an alcohol sodden co-ed. Each had their turn.

She tried thrashing weakly, but to no avail.

Turning, holding on to the steering wheel, looking out the side window, Jesse said, "You guys finished?"

"Yeah," Clint said.

"My turn then," Jesse said as he opened the door and quickly shut it. Going around the front of the car he reached the passenger door and flung it open, pulling Clint out of the car.

"Shut the door," Jesse commanded. Clint obeyed and stood outside looking at Jerry. Then he scanned the area.

"Scott, get out and shut the door quick."

Scott did so, quickly.

Jesse found panties and wiped between her thighs with it. Then he entered her and roughly raped her. "You sexy wench." It took him two minutes because he wanted to savor the moment. When he finished, he told Clint to throw her shoes across the railroad tracks into the weeds.

"Put her pants on," Jesse said.

Jerry and Scott climbed into the back and went to work. Clint got back into the front passenger seat. Jesse went around to the driver's side and jumped in.

He didn't want to see anything—stroking his conscience, he thought, *I'm just the driver.* "You guys ready to go?"

"We're trying to put her pants on."

"Hurry up. I'm getting out of here." He backed the car a few feet, turning the steering wheel, then slowly moved toward the highway. He bounced over the slight curb, hung a left, then turned on his lights and stepped on the gas. Made a left onto the dog leg road and over the train tracks then back through the sleeping streets of St. Helena.

Holding Elizabeth's panties up Scott said, "We didn't get her panties back on."

"Throw 'em out the window. And make sure her shoes are gone."

The others said yeah together in a low voice, coming off the after-sex languor. Not one of them showed or spoke about the crime they just committed. Jesse spoke, "How're you guys feeling?"

"Great," Clint said without enthusiasm.

Jesse himself felt great, smoking, enjoying the wind blowing through the Chevy. "Okay guys, here's the skinny. We got to dump her."

"Where?' Scott asked.

Jesse said, "Somewhere on Dundalk Avenue. Someone should see her. Anyone use skin?"

"There wasn't time and I didn't have one," Jerry said.

"Shit, Jesse, no one thought of that," Clint said, discomfort in his voice.

"Don't worry guys, it's a milkshake in there anyway." Jesse laughed.

Jesse drove Dundalk Avenue and slowly stopped at the traffic light at Dundalk and Liberty Parkway. Clint opened the door and leaned forward while Scott pushed the seat up leaning his back into it. He and Jerry struggled to get Elizabeth into a position where they pushed her out sideways.

"Hurry up, you dopes, there's cars coming," Jesse hollered.

Betty stumbled onto the street as they pushed her out. She fell to her knees hard enough to rip a hole on the left knee of her pants.

"She's out, man," Scott said.

Jesse picked up speed while Betty crawled and struggled to stand.

Betty stood wobbling, her head throbbing, dazed, drunk, and barefooted, she started to walk not realizing or remembering anything. Shaking, she crossed Liberty Parkway and Willow Spring Road where they met and crossed with Dundalk Avenue. After crossing the streets, she stumbled along the sidewalk in front of nearly new 1947 built brick apartments. Something seemed familiar with these apartments to her. Feeling that she had lived somewhere around here before. She somehow managed to pass the first row of seven doors without falling. She zigged and zagged onward. At the end of the second section of seven apartment doors she couldn't go any more. So she walked up to the last apartment's front first step, plopped down and pushed herself to a sitting position. Then she leaned back sideways on the other two steps. She moaned slightly. No one came out—not at three in the morning.

Cruising on his black 1963 Honda Dream 305, with gray fenders and chrome pipes, Freddy Ragsdale drove his motorcycle slowly on Dundalk Avenue. Freddy noticed a car about three quarters of a mile away on the other side and slowed down for a couple of seconds at the traffic light, then it picked up speed. Fifteen seconds later it roared past him and he thought he recognized the Super Sport and its driver. He pulled over to the curb and debated on whether to follow them. Turning the bike around he decided to follow. He gunned it. He caught them at a red light and pulled alongside and yelled, "Have you guys seen Betty Crenshaw?"

"Don't know her," Jesse said. All the windows were down because when you're cruising, that's cool. Everyone did that.

Someone from the back seat said, "Last time I saw her she was at Abby's party."

"Who're you?" Freddy asked.

Jesse spoke, "None of your beeswax, drape."

The light changed and Jesse sped off.

Freddy just sat there with the engine idling. "I know that guy in the backseat. Scott Turner. Shit!"

He turned the bike around and sped back to where he thought he saw Jesse's car slowed down. He parked the bike next to the curb. A car went by. He grabbed his flashlight out of his small saddlebag and searched the area. He spotted what looked like bloody footprints. *Strange.* He parked the motorcycle and scanned, then walked a little on the sidewalk. A little further on he spotted another one. It looked like they might be leading to those apartments that were up ahead.

He trotted back, jumped on his motorcycle and kick started it. With the engine idling, he lumbered toward the apartments using his legs and feet to move him along the road. A car passed him. The small 4-unit apartments had three stairs leading to a front door. He couldn't believe his eyes. He had missed seeing her when he left the Super Sport because he was on the other side of the avenue. Betty was laying on her side on the steps. Quickly he turned the bike off and ran up to her.

"Betty, are you okay?"

Dazed, Betty looked at him. "Huh."

"Where're your shoes?'

"Shoes." She smiled. "Freddy."

He helped her up. "Come on, I'll take you home."

They walked to his bike. "I can walk," Betty complained.

"Okay, can you get on my bike behind me?"

"Sure. I'm no cripple." She got on behind him and wrapped her arms around his waist.

Freddy revved the motorcycle and hurried off making a right onto Thruway. He came up on Willow Spring Road and made another right. A short sprint and he quickly made a left onto Keyway. Immediately passing Kinship he banged a right onto her street, Slowship Road. Finally reaching her house a quarter mile away. She was coming out of it, but she would not remember the ride to her house. She also didn't remember going inside.

Ragsdale helped her off and led her up the stairs to her front door. Freddy knocked on the door at Betty's house and her mother answered it.

"Oh my God, Betty! What happened?"

"I found her sitting on the steps of an apartment on Dundalk. The ones close to the Seagram's distillery. I don't know what happened but she's pretty soused." Freddy handed her off to her mother.

"Thanks, Freddy, we'll talk to you later." She pushed him out.

"But Misses Crenshaw..." The door slammed.

3

"What happened Betty?" asked her mother.

Betty shrugged her shoulders and smiled.

"It's three-thirty!" her father yelled as he rounded the corner from the kitchen to the living room. "What the hell happened to you?"

Betty smiled and shrugged her shoulders.

"You slut, I know what happened. You were drinking and had sex, didn't you!"

She smiled with droopy eyes.

The stucco row houses on Slowship Road were built in the early 1920s with walls made out of wood strips and mortar—solid and strong, but not totally soundproof.

Rayder went berserk and grabbed her hair and pulled her to the solid wall and banged her head against it. Betty just laughed. He slapped face and went down to the basement. Her sisters were peeking from the steps with tears rolling down their cheeks. Her mother went to her and held her.

"Come on, we'll clean you up a little. We're going to the police once you sober up some."

An hour later they were at the Dundalk Precinct of the Baltimore County police, down at the end of the block from the Strand movie theater. A uniform and a detective greeted them.

"I'm Detective Al Moss and this is Sergeant Casmir Dombrowski. How can we help you?"

"My daughter has been assaulted and raped."

"Come with us."

Betty and her mother were led to a small private room used as an interrogation room. The police sat behind the table and Frances and Betty sat opposite.

"Betty, can you tell us who assaulted you?" Detective Al Moss asked.

"I don't remember."

Moss frowned slightly. "Do you remember who gave you the alcohol?"

"I think it was a guy named Jesse."

"You think?"

"No, I remember his name was Jesse."

"Jesse who?" Casmir Dombrowski asked.

Detective Moss glanced at her mother.

"I don't know his last name. I never saw him before. He was old. Twenty or twenty-two, I think."

Nobody smiled.

Detective Moss asked, "If we showed some photos would you be able to pick out someone?"

Detective Moss nodded to Sergeant Dombrowski—he left the room.

"I don't know, I was pretty much under the weather. Don't remember anything."

Frances had been holding her hand and now she squeezed it slightly. Betty looked at her.

"I'm sorry mom."

Tears formed in Frances' eyes and she hugged Betty.

"Would either of you like some coffee or water?"

"No thank you, detective." Sniffling, Frances answered for both.

The sergeant came back in with a box. He put them in front of Moss. Moss went through it pulling out photos and preparing them face up.

"I have twenty mug, uh, photos here. Look at them carefully, one at a time. Take a good look at each one and take your time. There's no rush. Okay?"

Betty nodded her head yes.

He laid the first one down. Betty shook her head no. As he laid each one down side by side, Betty either said no or shook her head no or shrugged her shoulders.

"Look over them again to make sure." Moss encouraged.

With a slight sigh detective Moss looked at Frances and said, "Without any I.D.s we can't do anything."

Betty went through them again and still no recognition of any of the rapists.

Frances looked at Betty. "Didn't you say you were going to Abby's house?"

Betty nodded.

"Where does Abby live?" the sergeant asked.

"I don't know the address but I know how to get there."

"Is it in Dundalk?" detective Moss asked.

"It's across Dundalk Avenue in Saint Helena's."

"Know the street?" asked Sgt. Dombrowski.

"No. I never paid any attention."

"Were the ones who did this to you, there?"

"I don't remember. I think so. But I was pretty high when I first got there. No big deal."

Moss and Dombrowski noticed a shocked look on Frances' face. She opened her mouth and put her fist in it.

"I do remember that Jesse guy bringing in booze and..."

"Go on," Dombrowski said.

"I think he had three, four or five guys with him."

Al Moss asked, "Do you remember any other names besides Jesse?"

"There was one that hung around me. I remember taking a drag off his cigarette."

Her mother gasped.

"Oh mom, I bet you smoked behind the barn."

"Well…"

"Ladies, I'm trying to conduct an investigation. Betty, do you remember the guy's name?" Moss asked.

"I think he said." She looked up to her left. "His name was…Clit."

Moss and Dombrowski looked at each other. Moss questioned, "Clit? Are you sure?"

"No, but it was something like that."

Dombrowski was going to say something smart aleck but decided against it. Moss wrote the name down with spaces between letters. Dombrowski leaned over. Moss started to put in letters, trying vowels first. Didn't work. Then he went to consonants. "I don't think you can have three consonants in a row," Dombrowski said. "So…"

"So, what about Dombrowski? You have two sets."

He sat back. "It's all yours, Al."

"This is a short name." Moss got his point across.

"Are we finished?" Frances asked.

"No!" they said together.

Moss went back to work. "No consonants would make sense in front of the i, so let's put them behind the i."

He tapped the space behind the i and mentally placed some letters. He then wrote some down, crossing off the improbable; ~~Cligt~~, Clift, ~~Cliht~~, ~~Clikt~~, ~~Climt~~, Clint. "Okay, I think I have something…I hope. Does one of these ring a bell? Clift."

"Sounds like it might be," Betty said.

"How about Clint?"

"Yes! That's the one." She frowned. "I think."

"Okay. I think that will be all for today," Moss said. "We can't do anything with her unless she gives us something. Take her home, let her sleep and maybe she'll remember something." He put the pictures back into the box, then stood. He thought for a second, *the photos are men in their twenties.* "Just a second. Betty, how old were these men? Can you guess?"

"I guess they were around my age, sixteen, seventeen."

Dombrowski said, "Juvies."

"Would you say classmates?" Moss asked.

"Maybe. I don't know. Can't remember."

Looking at Frances he said, "Guys like these clowns prey on girls who drink and go to parties or clubs like Unity Hall, looking for their chance. A lot of them keep doing this for years until they slip and get caught. Most don't."

Frances looked at him askew.

"Most don't get caught is what I mean. For some high schoolers, it's their only time. For others, they do it again or get a criminal record." Al Moss continued, "Bring her back when she remembers. I'd like to get these bas, uh, guys before they do it to someone else. If we get this Jesse guy and he doesn't talk, he'll only get a year in jail or probation for giving minors alcohol."

Frances Crenshaw stood, tears running down her face, holding Betty around her shoulders. Sniffling she said, "Thank you detective. I'll bring her back if she remembers."

After they left Al said "Shit. High school boys." He told Dombrowski, "Go to the high school and get a list of all the boys' names. I mean all, in every grade."

"Today's Saturday, now," Casmir said looking at his watch then the calendar.

"Call the principal later in the morning. We have his home number."

"On Saturday?"

"I don't care if it's doomsday. Call later this morning."

When they got home Betty's sisters were watching TV.

"Where's dad?" Mom asked.

"Upstairs." Della answered.

"What happened?" Lizz asked.

"Nothing," Mom said. "You girls go up to bed."

"Aw, mom," Karen complained.

"Get up there now. Go, go, go!"

They all slowly climbed the stairs.

"Go take a shower Betty then you can sleep on the cot in the basement. You won't be bothered by your sisters. We'll talk later this morning about changing schools."

"I don't want to change schools. It's not my fault."

"We'll talk in the later. Go take a shower."

Saturday morning came late for Betty. As she lay in bed, she heard someone come down the stairs.

"I see you're finally awake. It's ten-thirty," her mother said.

"I must have needed the sleep."

Frances sat on the bed looking down at her daughter.

"I can't believe you did that," Frances said.

"Yeah, too much wine. No more wine for me—ever."

"That's part of it. Too much wine and you were an easy target for those bad boys, like Detective Moss said."

"I didn't ask for that to happen."

"In a way you did. You drank too much, too young to drink, of course boys hone in on that. The bad boys. You put yourself into that position and they jumped at it."

"Oh, so it *is* my fault," Betty snapped.

"Pretty much, so I'm thinking we'll get you started in another school."

"No! I'm not running. I'll face them. I don't care what they think! I'm not going to another school. My friends are here."

"You stay and you'll see how many friends you have. Nobody will talk to you."

"Abby will. Lexi will. And a couple of others."

"Betty, you'll lose most of your so-called friends."

"I don't care. I'm not changing schools."

Betty and her mother went back to the Police station after lunch. Detective Moss was there and he got the box of photos. They went through the same 20 and a few more. He knew it was useless but he wanted to be sure. Betty didn't recognize any of them.

"Misses Crenshaw, we called the principle this morning and he was good enough to give us a few names." He turned to Betty. "I'll say a name and tell me if you recognize them." He won't give the photos to go with the names—yet. If she recognizes a name, he'll get the photo.

He started off with Clinton Baxster. He didn't know but Baxster was black.

"No." Betty sat straight and had her hands folded on the table.

"Clifton Gallagher."

"No."

"Clint Zabinski."

"No."

"Clint Green."

"No."

Moss was very disappointed and it showed. That was all the Clint's or close to Clint from all three grades. Moss stood. "Thank you for coming."

As they turned to leave Moss said, "Wait. One more thing. Can you show us where—he looked at his notes—Abby lives?"

Betty looked at her mother and Frances said, "Yes."

They pulled up in front of Abby's house and all four got out of the unmarked black Ford. Moss knocked on the door. Mr. Beecher answered.

"Can I help you…officers?"

Moss said, "Yes. We'd like to talk with your daughter for a moment, just for information." He added, "She's not in trouble."

"If she's not in trouble why talk to her?"

Moss thought, good ol' daddy protecting his kid before he knew anything. "Like I said, she might have some information that might help this couple."

Mr. Beecher looked over Moss's shoulder. "I don't know them."

"I could come back with a court order than the whole world will know," Moss bluffed.

Beecher gave up. "Come on in."

Once inside the house the police notice Abigail Beecher appeared nervous and her parents looked puzzled and dismayed. Frances and Betty stood behind Moss and Dombrowski.

"Misses Beecher, Betty was at a party here yesterday evening. And we need some information that might help us with a situation."

"What kind of situation? Abby did you have a party here while we were gone?" Mr. Beecher asked.

"Not really. I just had a few friends over for cokes and music. We danced."

"How many…" Mr. Beecher started to ask but Moss chimed in.

"How many kids did you have over?"

"I guess it was four of us girls and four boys."

Abigail's mother had to sit down on the sofa with her hand to her heart.

"Did you know the boys?" Moss asked.

"Not really."

"You had boys in the house while we were gone and didn't know them!" Mr. Beecher hollered.

"Mister Beecher please sit next to your wife," Moss ordered.

Mr. Beecher wasn't finished. "I ought to whip…"

"Sir! Take a seat or I'll have to take your daughter to the station for questioning."

Mr. Beecher sat, fuming. Frances and Betty held each other near the front door.

"You don't remember any of their names?"

"No," she lied. She thought she was protecting her friend, like she should have Friday night.

"What about the girls?"

"We were all drinking and everything's hazy."

"You lying snot!" her father yelled.

"Mr. Beecher, last warning," Moss said.

Abby's mother laid back on the sofa clutching her chest.

"There was this older guy named Jesse who brought the wine."

"Jesse who?"

"No one knows his last name," Abby said.

Moss looked at Dombrowski, then he said, "If you remember anything give us a call, okay? Abby, we're here for you. When you're ready. Okay?"

"Yes, officer. I will."

Back at the station with the Crenshaws gone, Dombrowski said, "First it was cokes, then wine. She'll never come."

Moss shook his head. "I know. We have nothing. It's up to them. This is how this crap keeps happening." He threw his pen across the room.

"I wonder what the parents are gonna do?" Dombrowski asked.

"They better be careful. I don't want to throw them in jail for child abuse." Moss threw another pen across the room.

Betty stayed in that school and a few talked to her or looked at her curiously, except Abby and Mary. Later as a Senior, she had a few more friends. Memories are short for some people.

A week after the police interview, walking by herself during class change, she saw a boy walking towards her, staring into her eyes as they passed each other. She didn't know his name but she thought that he could be one of the guys because she remembered the eyes…those eyes.

She didn't know him—it was Clint Zabinski.

Scott Turner passed notes to his fellow criminals as they passed each other in the halls during class changing. The note said: *Meet me after school in Mars parking lot.* Mars was a popular grocery store on the corner of Delvale and Holabird Avenues not far from the High School.

Everyone was there except Jesse. Scott would have to get to him later. They went to the side of the store and all lit up cigarettes.

"I got youze guys here cause we're gonna make a pact. No one talks, no one snitches about what happened. Get the pix-chur?"

"Yeah, but what if the police come?" Jerry asked.

"You don't know nothing. Got it. It wasn't you. It wasn't us." Scott took out a switchblade and sprung it open. "Anyone talks and I will take care of you. Get it."

Everyone said yes to the young hood.

"We'll keep in touch by phone. Give me your numbers."

Clint held back.

"You too, Flint."

"I don't know, Scott."

"Look, Flint, you're in…like Flint."

Jerry laughed, "That's right, Flint."

Clint relented and gave his number. They all shook hands on it. Scott made sure they stayed in touch for decades. He had plans for his life. He had too much to lose.

The next day Scott found Jesse at *Mel's Package Goods* store. Mel's was like all of the other package goods stores—buy, take home liquor on one side and a bar on the other side; accessible through an open doorway. He found Jesse sitting at a table in the bar. Jesse looked up, twitched slightly. Surprise on his face, he said, "Scott ol' buddy. What's happening?"

Before Scott could say anything, Mel walked up.

"Hey kid. You gotta leave, unless he's your pa."

Scott glared at Mel and spoke to Jesse. "Let's go outside."

"I'll be there after I finish my beer."

Now Scott glared at Jesse. "Now!" He turned and walked out.

Jesse gulped his beer and followed seconds later.

Outside Jesse said, "What the heck is the matter with you? I've got a good mind to…"

"Shut up! Let's walk."

Jesse followed Scott a step behind him until they turn a corner into an alley. Scott stopped abruptly and Jesse Delaney bumped into him. Scott Turner shoved him away. "Listen, we all made a pact to keep our mouths shut about that night."

"Yeah. What's that got to do with me?"

"You're involved so you're in the pact."

"I ain't in no pact or pack, kid."

Before Jesse realized it, Scott had him up against the wall with his switchblade poking his throat. They were about the same height but Scott was muscle, Jesse, almost skin and bones.

"Listen, jerk, you screwed her like we all did. Keep your trap shut or I'll come after you. Give me your telephone number. I'll be checking on you every few months, like I will with the others."

"Sure, sure. That's groovy. Put that knife away and I'll give it to you."

After they parted and went their separate ways, Jesse thought, *that dork thinks he can control me. I'll have to set him straight.*

A couple of months later the 16-year-old Scott had to beat 20-year-old Jesse to a pulp because he smart mouthed Scott. Jesse now paid attention. After that, Jesse started to drink more often. No more big shot.

Scott Turner kept his promise and called them every 8 to 12 months—every year. Turner never trusted them, always fearful someone would rat, even after he retired from the Bethlehem Steel Mill in Sparrows Point, Maryland—known by the locals as the Point.

4

Twenty-four-year-old Karl Kephart walked into Squire's Café/Restaurant on Holabird Avenue with a couple of his friends. At five foot and eleven inches he was the tallest of the three men. His light brown hair, bleached by the sun, made his brown eyes stand out. All were built muscular with slightly weathered skin. They were from Oklahoma and came to Maryland to meet with potential beef buyers. The other two were also in their twenties. Steve, twenty-three and Bill was twenty-six, and all had their own cattle ranches that they inherited, coincidently within the same year when their fathers died. Each one had their mother living in a separate house close to the "big" house. They never knew each other until they were forced into the cattle raising business. They became close friends but very distant neighbors. Karl had his ranch north west of El Reno, Oklahoma. One of his friends was fifty miles away and the other was one hundred and ten miles away.

Today was Karl's lucky day. He spotted her almost as soon as he walked in—his future wife. She sat with two other girls.

Karl led the guys to a table close to them. He smiled at Betty after the waitress took their order. She smiled back.

Karl glanced at Betty and found her attractive, at least twenty-one, with shoulder length sun-streaked brown hair leaving highlights of blonde and a shapely athletic build. She also had a tan which complimented her yellow short skirt and modest white blouse.

Karl kept glancing at Betty and now noticed they all were drinking beers, so at the least, twenty-one. He also noticed they were about finished with their beers. He motioned the waitress over.

"Give the three ladies a refill on me."

She returned shortly to deliver the beers to the women. Betty lifted the glass to Karl and winked. Karl got up and lifted his chair over to them.

"Mind if we sit with you ladies?" He stood there, grinning.

"All you have to do is sit," Clara said.

"Thankee, ma'am," Karl said.

The other two guys followed with their chairs and said thankee also.

"So where are you gentlemen from?" Clara asked. *You called us ladies, I'll call you gentlemen.*

"Oklahoma, ma'am," Bill said.

All together the women said, "Tornado alley."

Everyone laughed. "You all get some tornados here," Karl smiled.

"Yeah, but not like yours," Betty countered. "Not every year."

The men let that go by and Bill started the intros. "Well, I'm Bill, Ladies."

"I'm Steve."

"Excuse my manners, I'm Karl."

"I'm Betty and she's Clara. The brunette is Donna."

The waitress arrived to take an order.

"How about we order a very large meat, onion and mozzarella pizza," Karl said.

Everyone agreed.

While eating, the guys—well mostly Karl, told them about their business trip to supply restaurants in the area with Grade A Oklahoma beeves.

When everyone got up to leave together Karl took Betty aside and asked if he could see her again. She hesitated.

"Here, I'll give you my hotel room phone number," Karl offered.

"Okay, but I can't promise anything. My job is working overtime but today we took off."

"Where do you work?"

"We all work at Eastern Electric. It's a factory job."

"No shame in that. Pays good, I bet."

"Yes it does. How long will you be in Dundalk?"

"We're staying in Baltimore but will be all around the area, so we don't know until we get enough firm commitments to buy."

"Well then, I'll call you." Betty stuck out her hand. "Thanks for the beers and pizza, cowboy."

Karl took her hand, bent down and kissed it. "My pleasure Betty." At that moment Betty's heart fluttered and knew then, he would be her wealthy cattle and horse baron husband.

"My, such chivalry in nineteen seventy."

"We are like that in Oklahoma."

They looked at their clasped hands, separated them, and laughed.

"I'll call you," Betty said.

Then each group went to their cars, smiling, waved and drove off.

Karl and Betty started dating every day for the next week. When he went back to Oklahoma, he called every day; expensive but he thought she was worth it. He flew her to Oklahoma twice for a week's stay each time. She loved Oklahoma. Wide open spaces, fewer people—and no one knew her past.

On his fifth trip back to Maryland—since meeting her and it being a non-working trip—he proposed to her and she excitedly accepted. Six months after the proposal they were married in her Methodist church in Dundalk.

She thought that finding a person from Oklahoma, and moving there, she wouldn't have to worry about bumping into someone that might know about the incident, as she called it. She would never see any of her old classmates.

Over five decades later Betty suddenly remembered that rape. The aftermath of rape, the police interview, the trauma, home, and the looks from classmates. No one knew the trauma she went through and the crying, sleepless nights. She had put up a good front. That was it. A front only, no therapy. Especially back then.

Karl and Betty had an argument when they saw one of the President's nominee was being slandered on TV. She had remembered the rape because of the *Me Too Movement*, brought up by the hearings. She felt scared and vulnerable again.

Karl was angry at the proceedings they were watching on their smart Samsung TV. He said, "I remember in my late teens and early twenties about three different girls I dated told me on the first date, mind you, that they were virgins, oh, except they were raped once. Yeah right, I thought. Gave them an excuse, I guess, to get some action. Never dated them again. And I didn't do anything with them. Rape indeed."

"They probably told the truth," Betty said.

"What, back in the mid to late sixties?"

"Yes, the beginning of free love and boozing and marijuana and LSD. Remember?" She remembered and now felt sick to her stomach—keeping that secret.

Sadly, he nodded his head—he remembered alright. In his late teens and early twenties, he'd regularly accompanied his father on buying/scouting trips as his father called them. They'd drive or fly to Kansas City, Chicago,

Columbus, Washington, D.C., Baltimore City, Philadelphia, and sometimes to New York City to drum up sales for their beef. They always left home with a list of restaurants and meat markets to canvas and make sales.

In the evenings Karl would go to the clubs, dance halls, or wherever there were women to be found. In Dundalk it was Unity Hall that was the place to be. Just for fun—he wasn't looking for a wife then.

Yeah, things were pretty open and loose then. Even more so today.

"I was raped once," Betty spoke softly.

With a surprised look on his face Karl asked, "What are you talking about?"

"When I was sixteen, I was raped after a party at my girlfriend's house."

"You were raped at your girlfriend's house?"

"No. I was drunk and some guys somehow got me into their car."

"You're seventy-one now and just remembering this?" Karl asked gently.

"Yes, I've suppressed it down into a deep hole. Now this crap comes up on TV and some of it comes tumbling back." She paused. "I had been to a party that my friend had at her house and drank too much and was raped," she blurted out quickly.

"Where? At the party?" Karl couldn't believe his ears. Though he wasn't a virgin or a libertine, he thought he married a virgin. And she never let on that she wasn't—of course.

"No. I said, in the car."

"You couldn't stop him?"

"No. I was too drunk. I don't remember hardly anything except that it was more than one."

Karl felt gut punched. "More than one what? How many times?"

"I don't know. It was multiple."

"Multiple what? Times?"

"Multiple guys."

"What! How many?"

"I don't know. I don't REMEMBER!"

"You don't remember?!"

Angrily she said, "Look, I don't want to talk about it."

"Can you identify them?"

"I said I don't want to talk about it. No, I can't remember them."

Betty got up and went into the farthest bathroom and shut the door.

Karl thought he was about to puke. He started pacing the living room, then the den, then back to the living room. *She brought it up.* He pounded his fist into his palm. "I want those sons a bitches!"

He didn't know what to do, or how to handle this situation—yet. It was a long silent night for both of them.

Karl tried to find out more details the next day but the chances of that were slim to none—and slim was out of town. He finally convinced Betty to talk…a little. Betty thought they went to her high school but wasn't sure. He got out her yearbooks and made her go through them and came up with one maybe—finally. She only remembered that she told the police a guy named Jesse got the alcohol for them. She said she told the police another name but nothing came of it.

"What was his name?"

"I DON'T remember!"

He didn't know what to do but he wouldn't forget it. He couldn't forget it. Then he figured out what to do. He would call his friend, Lance Pruitt. He should know something about how to find people. Or he knows people who can.

5

He wore a light brown short sleeve shirt, khaki pants, and brown hiking shoes. His legs were spread as he lay on the light golden long-stemmed weeds in between two clumps of brush. The familiar odor of grass, dirt, and the Pacific made him feel comfortable, like he belonged there. Thickets of trees and brush surrounded him and he felt fairly well hidden from view of anyone or anything. He was bare headed, having laid his light green cap beside him. "Get away from me, damn gnat." Jake Baer had no time to swat it.

The sun's warmth penetrated through his blonde whiffle, as he called it; old slang for a crew cut or military cut styled hair. Focusing on his job, his vivid cobalt blue eyes squinted through the Leupold 10x scope as he adjusted the knobs for windage and distance. He readjusted his legs, now only slightly apart, on his 5 feet 11-inch, full frame of a weightlifter.

His specially modified, M24 Sniper Weapons System free floating barrel rested on its bi-pod. The bolt action Remington had a fully loaded five round magazine attached to it. Jake Baer planned on using just two rounds of the 7.62x51mm NATO X—if things went according to plans. X meant it was an exploding bullet. On impact.

Using night vision goggles, Baer had smuggled and hid his equipment at that spot last night, in the trees, not far from Gate Vista Point parking area.

That morning he used the parking lot and blended in with a few scattered walkers taking photos from the Point's height. He walked a seldom used trail then veered off. When he neared his spot, he veered off again at an angle.

Interstate 280/Junipero Serra Freeway, had its normal pack of vehicles travelling beyond the posted speed limit. He picked a white car to his right travelling south at, he guessed, seventy-five miles per hour and followed it, moving himself and the barrel right and followed it moving now to his left, swiveling on the bi-pod. He saw the driver clearly and made another slight adjustment to the scope.

"Target just passed me at approximately seventy mikes an hour," chirped his spotter's voice in his ear bud. "Travelling in the slow lane."

"Copy," Jake Baer replied. That meant the black, and tinted windows, of the California Highway Patrol car Pablo Goliad occupied was now less than two miles away. He had only seconds to prepare and swung the SWS to his right. Again, he had to compensate for the wind that came from the south at fifteen miles an hour, using Kentucky windage. He also had to compensate for a moving target going in the opposite direction, into the wind.

The ChiPs' car had left San Francisco's County Booking and Release Center Jail #1, earlier. Pablo Goliad was being transferred to San Mateo County Jail in Redwood, CA. to wait until his time to be turned over to Federal Agents for deportation for the sixth time. The police thought I-280 would be safer than the 101.

This sucker murdered a thirty-two-year-old woman in 2015, 5yrs ago and got away with it. Claimed he found the gun, that had been stolen from a Federal Bureau of Land Management agent, under a bench at the beach. He had fired the gun "accidentally". Baer turned his head to spit.

"There you are", he whispered, as the car appeared around the bend. "You black hearted sucker."

The barrel followed until the car was right in front of Jake. He again used Kentucky windage to lead the car because of the blowing south wind.

CHAPTER 5

Over a thousand-meter shot. Taking in a deep breath and slowly exhaling he squeezed the trigger. The report was muffled somewhat by the silencer.

Baer saw the rear tire behind the driver explode, then shred. The driver fought to control the swerving car. Quickly the patrolman pulled to the shoulder and stopped. Both front doors opened together and two uniformed ChiPs' exited. They looked at the damaged tire and one kicked it, then went to the trunk and opened it. The other went to the back door, looked around and up at the hill across the Interstate. The hill that Baer was hiding on. Then he opened the door and motioned for his charge to get out. Through the scope Baer confirmed it was Goliad, hands cuffed behind his back. The target was at a greater distance than when he fired the first shot. He put the cross hairs on one dot left of Goliad's head, and one dot up, compensating for the wind and drop of the bullet so he could hit the spot between his eyes. He drew in a breath and slowly let it out and squeezed the trigger. Goliad's face exploded with blood, brains and flesh splattering the officer.

Knowing it was a good kill, Bear quickly broke down the 24-inch barrel from the Remington stock by turning three butterfly screws close to the trigger. Stuffing the stock, barrel, and screws into his backpack, then he grabbed the two empty casings on the ground and put them in his pockets. He looked to make sure his spot was clean and fluffed up some branches. Then Baer threw the pack on his back and nonchalantly walked the 1300 feet back to his car, saying hi to a couple that passed him. No one heard or saw anything unusual.

"Fuck the tire! Call it in!" The officer bent over the illegal's lifeless body and said, "I don't feel sorry for you, wetback." He looked around and then up again toward the west to the hills. "You got him good, whoever you are." He had his pistol pointed down and away from his leg. He knew it was a long shot, making his weapon useless. He assumed they were in no danger or they would be dead by now. He walked to the front of the car shaking his head. Holstering his pistol, he murmured, "Sure made us look bad." He leaned on the front fender to wait for the Calvary.

Within a half hour the Highway Patrol had the Interstate's right lane closed. More officers and a helicopter were combing the area they thought the shot might have come from. It took them an hour to get to the spot where Baer had been, walked by it, noticing nothing out of place. After two hours they gave up, and no one saw or heard anything.

After Baer had put his equipment into a rented storage unit, using a false I D, he wiped everything clean wearing latex surgical gloves. Then he drove the rental south to Los Angeles and stopped for lunch. Afterwards he headed south again toward the San Diego International Airport to catch a pre-arranged non-stop flight on a private jet because of the on and off and on Corona virus outbreaks. The private owner, nor the pilots knew his real name or what he did for a living. They flew him to Dulles Airport in Chantilly, Virginia. He lived in Virginia where he moved, after living in Oklahoma City for a few years. Former Oklahoma Senator John Smithe, now fully retired, decided to stay permanently in Great Falls, Virginia and the senator wanted to have Baer close by. Baer lived in Shady Oak, Virginia, a hop, skip, and a jump away, as one of Smithe's geeks would say.

Once Baer got home, he grabbed a cold one out of the fridge, watched a little of Newsmax on TV to catch up on any news, then he went to bed.

The spotter, Robert Rocke, a former Navy Seal, had disappeared immediately into the realm of the soldiers of fortune world to wait for someone else needing his Salvage services. He drove his black Ford Expedition back to Florida. He liked to be in control of his destiny, plus he liked to drive—car or boat.

6

Lance Pruitt's phone chimed and he reached into his pocket to answer. "Hello Karl."

Karl Kephart had been a good friend of Pruitt's for a few years. Kephart, at seventy-three, was in excellent health, tanned, and strong, but felt weak calling Pruitt. He needed help with this situation and Pruitt knew how to keep his mouth shut. Plus, Pruitt had good connections for what he had in mind.

"Lance, would you come over? I need your advice on a delicate matter."

"Sure. Mind if I bring Angie?"

"I'd rather you not. This is personal and very private. Though it might become embarrassingly public."

"Uh, sure. No problem. I'll be right over."

"Thanks, my friend."

"Who was that?" Angie asked.

"Karl. Says he needs my advice on something."

"Like what?"

"Don't know but he wants it on the Q T."

"Probably some boring cowboy talk. I'll go back to my painting."

"What are you painting now? The library or the bedroom?" Lance teased.

"I was going to paint a landscape but now I think I'll do a portrait of you with freckles and buck teeth." Angie walked off smiling.

Lance hollered, "Make my teeth have a split in the front."

She yelled from her studio, "I'll do a good job."

He laughed. He loved his wife and would die for her. Though he hoped that would never happen.

They had moved back to the Town of Dry Creek after a few years of condo living in Oklahoma City. Lance was happy they moved back, even though living in the city with its new condos was enjoyable, it kept getting really crowded, especially since Scissortail Park opened. He knew about the plans to expand the park and other major projects, financed by a one percent sales tax added to the tax rate. The voters happily kept renewing that option. Still, he missed the open spaces—which were getting less and less. At least by Oklahoma standards.

Pruitt drove through the gates of Double K Bar Ranch. By Oklahoma standards, Karl didn't live too far from Lance. Karl met him at the door. They shook hands.

"Have a seat," Karl offered, extending an arm to a chair. The house was modest by wealthy Oklahoma standards. Lance took a seat in a leather high back chair.

"What can I do for you?" Pruitt asked.

"Betty isn't here right now. Shopping at Quail Springs Mall," Karl began.

"Okaaay." Pruitt said.

"It has to do with her. She blurted it out last week. The 'Me Too' movement jogged her memory and what I had said to her."

Pruitt looked apprehensive. "What did you say."

"Oh, we were talking about the good old days of the sixties and I brought up a couple of exploits."

"Oh, boy."

"We were kinda arguing about the dates we had, the girls were pretty easy to get along with...if you get my drift."

"Yes."

"But nothing like today. Anyway, I said it seemed like every other girl I took out told me, voluntary, mind you, that they were virgins. But…" He paused. "You want something to drink?"

"Beer's fine."

"Bull crap. You're having a whiskey sour like me." He smiled and walked to a small bar.

"Okay." What else could he say?

Karl handed the drink to Lance then sat with his.

"But they all said they were raped—once. My guess was, they thought if I had sexual relations with them, I wouldn't be surprised if I didn't pop their cherry."

Lance took a very long sip. He didn't say a word. Just let him get it off his chest. Karl stared at his drink. Then quickly emptied his glass.

"Want another?" he asked.

Lance shook his head. "Not yet. So, what's on your mind?"

"You're good friends with the police, right?" Karl went to the bar and filled his glass.

"I know some in Dry Creek, El Reno and Oklahoma City. Why?"

When he sat again, he said, "This is very private and hard for me to come to grips with. I need someone to check with the Dundalk, Maryland police about an incident that happened, maybe in late September, nineteen-sixty-five." He took a pull of his drink.

Lance leaned forward in his chair. "With you?"

"No, with Betty. She was sixteen at the time."

"Oh, shit. What happened?"

Karl told Lance everything he knew about "the incident", as he also called it.

"I'm sorry, Karl. That's beyond terrible. What a burden…poor Betty. And a burden for you, too. What do you want me to do?" He had finished his drink and spun the ice cubes in the glass.

"I need one or both police departments to call the Dundalk police and send me the report so I can press charges…after I find him, or them."

"What about the statute of limitations? Here they are home free after 10 or 20 years depending on the type of rape."

"I hear now there's no statute of limitations here. Anyway, I plan on doing it in Maryland. Maryland has no limitations for rape of any kind. The only good thing I know of that Maryland does right, except marrying us. That was good." Karl grinned.

"I didn't know you met her and married her in Maryland." He just learned something new about his friend. He never talked about being out of state, even once.

"I was on a business trip, with other sellers, to sell western cattle to a company headquartered in Baltimore. You know, for the meat and steak market, for restaurants, grocery stores, et cetera. After business we all went to an Italian Restaurant in Dundalk. Squire's it was called. Still there, I hear. Anyway, Betty was eating lunch there with a couple of her friends. Turns out we hit it off. I asked her out, after all of us finished eating. The men told me later on our way back to the motel that they were surprised she accepted."

"You must have made a real good impression."

"She couldn't resist my charm," he laughed. Then he grew serious. "She's a good woman and no one does that to my wife." Karl stared into Lance's eyes. "I want justice or their hide."

Lance held his glass out. "I think I'll have another."

As Karl walked to re-fill both glasses he remarked, "I'd like to see them dead…if I had my way."

Lance sat back and looked at the ceiling. He wasn't sure he should say what he was about to say—but he had no use for rapists. Vigilante justice? No, just justice. "That might be possible."

Karl looked back at him. "Are you kidding? That ain't gonna happen unless they get the death penalty. And that ain't a sure thing."

He walked back and handed Lance his drink. "It's not revenge that I want. I want retribution or justice. Whatever you want to call it. Just get them."

"Let me see what I can do. I might know some people. If they find the rapists, justice will be swift and final." Lance drank half his glass. *What the hell am I saying?*

"Don't you now let that whiskey get to your head and you do something dumb." Karl smiled.

"Let me back up. I'll see what I can do. I didn't say, *I* was going to do anything." His eyes bored into Karl's. "I should say, I might know some people who might know some people."

"Glad you said that. And I like what I heard. Just let me get the police report first. I want to kill the past."

"No problem," Lance assured and finished his drink. "But I have to tell you it will be expensive."

"I don't care if I go broke. I want swift justice. I don't care how it's done, nor do I want to know—as long as it's done. As a matter of fact, I'd like every one of the bastards strung up by their balls."

"I can guarantee, it will be done. You know, once it starts, I don't think we can stop it."

"Fine with me." Karl got up to fix another drink.

"Better fill mine up again."

"No, sir. You're driving and I don't want my contact ending up in a ditch dead, from a wreck."

Lance didn't argue. "Then I better get going and get it started." Lance stuck out his hand and Karl clasped it with both of his.

"Thanks my friend," Karl said.

7

Lance pulled into his garage and pushed the button to turn off the engine. He loved not having to use a key, except to lock it. Angie's car, a Corvette, was gone, which meant she was probably shopping. Gone too was the Thunderbird. Got a great price for it. He had pared down his vehicles to his 2020, black Mustang 5.0 and now, Angie's 2016 white 'Vette that he bought her.

He entered the house through the kitchen and moved down the hall to his office. He reached his desk, went around it and sat in his high back leather chair. He punched a speed dial button on his landline phone—didn't take any chances someone might be listening. His house was a totally dumb house; no electronics except for a special alarm system that Lewis and Clark installed. He felt safe in calling his old detective friend, Nick Witkowski, for advice.

"Nick, this is Lance."

"Yes, I know."

"Hey, it could have been Angie."

"She doesn't call on that number."

"Okay, okay, you ol' crank."

"I'm trying to put a puzzle together."

"You're in Florida, retired, and you're putting a puzzle together?"

"Yeah. I do this before I go play golf with the president."

Lance snickered. "I'm sorry I caught you at a busy time but I need some advice."

"I got plenty of that."

"A friend of mine, you know him, Karl Kephart, has a very bad situation."

"Don't we all."

"Heck, Nick, who pissed in your Wheaties today."

"Oh, I'm tired of being retired."

"Good."

Lance proceeded to tell him everything that Karl told him.

Nick's heart raced. Maybe he can do some police work with this. "Damn, Lance, sure I'll see what I can do. For starters, does he want justice, revenge, or see if the gang's still alive?"

"He wants a police report."

"He won't get one. There won't be one from what you told me."

"Okay. Then he said he wanted, quote, 'every one of the bastards strung up by their balls,' end quote."

Silence on the other end. Lance didn't say a word. He knew Nick was mulling it over. Finally, "Is he serious about that?"

"As a heart attack."

"I'll make a call. Do me a favor—that we will never talk about this to our wives or each other again. We'll be money exchangers only."

"No problem. Also, the expenses are no problem. And thanks."

They disconnected. Lance said to no one, "I don't know nuttin', say nuttin', see nuttin', hear nuttin.'"

The ex-senator of Oklahoma picked up on the second ring.

"Nick it's good to hear from you. How's Florida been treating you?"

"Good, 'cept it's scary during hurricane season. I'd rather dodge tornados."

"I hear, ya."

"John, I'm gonna tell you something for your ears only."

"Shoot."

"For one thing, I have a friend of a friend, who might need…no, who wants some wet work done."

"Tell me about it." Former Oklahoma Senator John Smithe had been out of office for a while but he still operated his clandestine problem-solving network. Headquartered out of and under his house in Great Falls, VA. Someone has a problem the law or nobody else can help with, he's the man to go to.

After Nick told what Karl said, without using Karl's name, the senator said, "Let me get this straight. His wife was raped by a group of teenagers back in sixty-five. Ages were sixteen to seventeen."

"Maybe an eighteen to twenty-year-old too, a Jesse." Nick said.

"Whatever. They were all juveniles, right?"

"I guess. All under twenty-one."

"So, they're in their early seventies now—if living?"

"That'll be my guess."

"And we have no names."

"Except the first name of the guy who bought the alcohol for the kids, Jesse." Nick sensed the senator was mulling it over.

"Was that recorded at the time?"

"I believe so, senator. The Baltimore County Police should have it on file. There is no Dundalk Police. There is a Dundalk Precinct of the Baltimore County Police. I know I should know better but I was hoping that the Dundalk precinct might still have it."

"Nick, my man, it's probably in a cardboard box buried deep inside a funky basement in an old building rented by the locals. The police started to put everything on computers in ninety-five. That's thirty years later, buried, and I don't think they're going to dig it up twenty-five years after that for one old woman's hazy memory. Fifty-five years is a long time. Plus, in Maryland, giving alcohol to a minor was a misdemeanor with a one-year statute of limitations. If it went to court it would only be like a year of whatever, fine, jail, community service."

Nick knew he had a point. "I know, that was about the time Oklahoma City started to put our info on computers. But I know Maryland doesn't have a statute of limitations for rape crimes."

"I know that. That's not the point. It's how do we find them? A booze pusher for the kiddies is not a high priority case. The Maryland police aren't exactly gung-ho over cold cases, much less one that's over fifty-five years cold. Baltimore County has one dedicated Sergeant for cold cases. Heck, Nick, you know Oklahoma City Police has one *retired* officer to work cold cases, in a very small closet office. They both have hundreds of backlogged cold cases."

Witkowski reminded Smithe of the obvious, "Senator you have the nerd twins and Quark. They should be able to do it. Even though I used to work for the Baltimore City police doesn't mean I have any influence with them."

The senator did have two investigators, Lewis, code named—Lewis, and Clark, code named—Clark, working in his underground facilities with their computers and, Quark, that Lance Pruitt sold to the ex-senator, some fifteen years ago. Quark was a quantum computer, called an atomic QC, that computed by using atoms.

They also had the capability to search the files and reports of various police department around the country. That's how the senator gave Nick the info about the Baltimore County cold-case officer. Clark had walked it up to Smithe three minutes ago. All phone conversations were recorded and listened to. They were kept or deleted as needed.

"Point taken. I'll get them working on it right away but we'll need more info," Smithe said.

Witkowski continued, "She does remember what one looked like. Tall, dark hair comb straight back, and dark piercing eyes. Graduated in sixty-seven. He flunked a grade but don't know which one. Should have *not* been in her class, but was. My friend can send a high school photo."

The senator coughed.

"Are you still on those nasty cigars?" Witkowski asked.

"No, doctor told me I had to quit. I'll get the geeks on this right away."

"Thanks. It means a lot to the Mister—and the Misses."

"Means a lot to me also. In this time of the 'Me Too' crowd I've been more aware of the plight of women, especially young vulnerable girls." The senator sounded truly concerned.

"Thanks, John. Remember, price is no problem."

"Don't worry about the price. We price our missions fairly. This info comes from the injured party directly to you?"

"No. I have to report to a go-between. Who will also go nameless."

"Good. That's very good. The more insulation the better. It's a go, Nick."

"Thanks. I'll let them know the good news," Nick said.

They hung up and Smithe immediately called Jake Baer.

"What's up, Senator?"

"Come over. I have an important job for you."

"I thought as much. Seems you never call socially."

Smithe let out a sigh. "When have you become a social butterfly?" Smithe pulled the phone away from his ear. Baer's laughter seemed to fill the room.

Between gulps of laughter Baer said, "Sorry, but you made my day."

"I've got something that might make your month. So, get a grip and listen."

"Sure, sure," Baer said as he came to seriousness.

"Come over here now, we need to talk in person."

"Sounds serious. Be right over." He hung up.

Smithe stared at the phone a second and put it in its cradle. All important calls were made on a landline.

He smiled. They had more of a father son relationship, than employer and employee. The Senator had "adopted" Jake Baer when Jake was in his teens. Jake came to the United States from Germany as an orphan. He had the trauma of witnessing his parents' murder by a Muslim jihadist. After a few months his relatives transported him to the United States to live with his uncle Todd Bear in Philadelphia, who had anglicized his name from Baer. Smithe had literally bumped into Jake Baer, catching him shoplifting. Smithe took an instant liking to the young man and being childless, he and his wife took Baer, by mutual agreement, back to Oklahoma with them. They "adopted" him shortly thereafter. Later Smithe was elected senator of Oklahoma and pulled strings to get him into the Navy Seal training without joining the Navy. Jake became a useful and willing tool for the senator, as well as for the country. He loved America and became a legal citizen.

Baer backed his non-descript Hyundai silver SUV, out of the garage of his mansion, with the darkest tinted windows as allowed by Virginia law, which wasn't much. He was headed toward Smithe's house. Glancing to his left at his neighbor's long three hundred feet driveway and the house that was ninety percent hidden by trees, he spotted a dog trotting toward the drive. Continuing down his street, he turned right onto Watershed Street. Since it was summer the trees hadn't their autumn colors yet to blaze out, and he loved the fall colors when the trees turned. Besides that, he liked the trees for privacy and living in Shady Oak wasn't too far from the senator's Great Falls mansion. Driving south through light traffic on state highway 681, he thought, *I hope it's another Muslim or illegal alien assignment. I loved that last assignment in San Francisco.*

His neighbors thought he established his residence here like everyone else who had high paying cushy jobs in the federal government—to get away from the rat race and the rats of the District. His job was to kill the rats in the race. He considered himself as a paladin or a garbage disposal.

He pulled onto the senator's driveway and parked close to the garage door. Pushing the remote button, he watched it roll up revealing senator John Smithe standing in front of his SUV, looking serious. He left his car and shut the door.

"Well you look bloody serious, John."

"It's going to be a serious business." Turning, Smithe walked into the house with Baer following. Leading Baer to the library he pointed to a chair and sat in one across from Baer. Squirming to get comfortable the senator said, "This is a tough one. It's a fifty-five-year-old cold case. We all will have to do some detective work, I'm sure."

"Why is that?"

"Because the victim doesn't remember a whole lot about what happened."

"What happened?"

Just then, Jeeves, the butler walked in. "Drinks, Senator?"

"Yes, two scotch on the rocks. Usual amount."

"Very good, sir." Jeeves left the room.

"Jeeves? What happened to Alfred?"

"Death in the family."

"Sorry to hear that." Baer said sympathetically. "Close family or relative?"

Smiling the senator said, "Yes. Himself."

Rolling his eyes Jake Baer sat back and crossed his legs European style. "Okay get to the case, which sounds like more work and investigating than last month's unfortunate *accident* with Pablo Goliad."

"Jeeves came highly recommended by the Royal Family. He's an authentic English gentlemen's gentleman."

Bear had to put up with the Senator's interrupting banter, which was usually worse with a hard to solve case. Sitting back, stretching his legs, Smithe crossed his ankles.

"Jake, my boy, this is about as dastardly as they come. A gang rape of a sixteen-year-old. Took advantage of her while she was highly intoxicated. In a car, by some railroad tracks, in Baltimore."

Jeeves arrived with the drinks, served them, bowed slightly and left.

"Your job is to find the boys—old farts now, and string 'em up by the balls."

"Literally?"

"That's what he wants, but your job is just kill them anyway you have to."

"Sounds like the long arm of the law never reached them." Taking a long pull of his drink, Baer finished half of it. "Wow. Damn, that's good." He set the glass down on the table next to him. "Let's get started then. Lewis and Clark here?"

They used the code names, Lewis and Clark for Smithe's computer geeks, when they searched for info. When trying to find the why and how answers to the searched people, places, or things, they used the help of their brothers, Holmes and Watson, in the NSA. The brothers at NSA were totally—dark. The senator knew all of their real names. Lewis and Clark both used to work for the NSA, but now full time with the senator.

"Yes, in the Underground."

"Let's go."

They took their drinks and walked through the dining room with its crystal chandelier glowing like a short fat stalactite. Then walked through the kitchen where Jeeves busied himself preparing the dinner meal for later. Baer said hi and Jeeves nodded. Reaching a solid wood door, just beyond the kitchen, Smithe unlocked it with the key he held in his hand. They went down a flight and a quarter, narrow stairs and at the bottom they stopped at a heavy steel bomb resistant door that had a hand identifying electronic lock. Placing his palm on the scanner pad they saw a green light flash and heard a click. Smithe pulled a handle towards him. They stepped through and Baer pulled it shut, locking it automatically. They entered a well-lit 25 x 30 room that was the now the home of Quark, the Quantum Computer.

This computer was a little larger than a regular home desktop computer. Extremely advanced for the very late nineties, that the Y2K "crisis" never affected it. The twenty-three-inch flat screen stand-alone monitor and a larger than normal Central Processing Unit, the brains, were the main physical features. Two, nine-and-a-half-inches high, Altec Lansing external speakers stood close by. The best thing about the computer seemed to be that it was still twenty years ahead of anything else, civilian or military. Quark could speak, hear, "see" everything, or so it seemed to the geeks. Quark never slept. One couldn't turn him off. They were still in awe of Quark. It was more powerful with its artificial intelligence "circuitry" that Quark beat all of the seven dwarves in the basement at Langley, the Cray computers.

In the last couple of years, Langley had added an eighth Cray super computer and they were still no match for Quark. It could hack into the Crays without leaving a trace and steal their classified information. Quark would get the info and backtrack to the Underground by bouncing off of at least seven satellites and some cables. Lewis and Clark also had five other computers, that weren't as good as the Crays, but they were almost there.

Only thing wrong with Quark was that it was an invalid. Quark couldn't move around on his own. Thank the heavenly pixies, Smithe would say.

Jacob Baer asked if Quark knew everything.

"Sure. He knows everything. I talked to him on my iPhone this morning," Smithe said.

Walking into the room, Baer was again impressed with the intelligence setup Smithe had under his house. Besides Quark and the five other modern computers, sat five flat screen monitors, land line telephones, printers, and other highly sophisticated equipment. Three large flat screen TVs hung on the wall. They were now in the bowels of Smithe's communication complex in his basement. Baer thought more powerful than the CIA and NSA put together. Lewis and Clark were sitting in their chairs working at the computers. A forty-eight-inch diameter round conference table and a four-drawer filing cabinet sat at the far end of the room. With the world situation getting worse, Smithe was considering getting another person to help the geeks.

"Hey guys, how's it hanging?" Greeted Baer.

"To the left," said Lewis.

Bear chuckled.

Clark kept working but mumbled, "Hi Jake."

Baer ask Smithe if one of the guys could explain the workings of Quark to him.

"Lewis, would you explain to Jacob how Quark thinks?"

"Sure. First off, instead of computer chips or integrated circuits, this Quantum Computer uses atoms. It's a billion times faster than a Pentium III PC or a personal computer. The atoms are natural tiny calculators, having a natural spin or orientation—the spin can be up or down."

Second, with digital technology, everything is represented by 0s and 1s. The atom's spin pointing up, can be 1, and down, can be 0. That's basically how it operates."

All Baer could say was, "That's simple enough. So simple a baby could understand it. But, after all, I'm no baby."

Clark let out a laugh.

Smithe had told Baer that The Underground needed a powerful computer like this. The latest and greatest gadget of all time. That's why he bought it from Pruitt— at Lewis and Clarks' insistence.

By Buying Quark, Smithe now was one of a handful of wealthy or influential people in the world with a Quantum Computer. He felt this was the beginning of the artificial intelligence era. No one could use this computer but the geeks. Not even the ex-senator. They programmed the

QC so the computer would allow only Clark or Lewis to activate it. It used face, voice, touch, and wave recognition.

Lewis waved the machine on. Then he typed in details on the heliograph keyboard, that lit up on his desk, details anyone else he could think of. It would also find murderers, kidnappers, and all other crooks faster and more, accurately.

When he finished typing, he spoke to the computer. "Quark, I have typed in some information."

Within seconds Quark said, "They have sealed Maryland juvenile records. I will have the information in ten seconds."

"Seems, you don't really need a keyboard," Baer said.

"Not really. Most times it's faster talking to Quark."

Quark printed out a hard copy of the question asked. Lewis retrieved it and handed it to Clark who was working on the Chinese buildup in the Pacific. Americans working for China. Traitors.

"Listen up guys." Smithe repeated the details of the sorted story to the "brothers", Lewis and Clark.

"Well, that's not much to go on," Lewis said.

"We'll tell Quark," Clark said.

"Quark, wake up!" yelled Clark, just to get a rise out of Quark.

You don't have to yell. I have been awake as you say, the whole time. I just gave you the details of the American spies for China. I heard your other verbiage and it is not enough information to give you a solid start. The information I have is that Fredrick, AKA Freddy, Ragsdale, who picked her up on his motorcycle died in twenty-oh-six. Clint Zabinski is living in Dundalk with a woman he's not married to. His wife died in twenty-fifteen. His three children, one male, two females have longer criminal records than he does. His is two citations for disorderly conduct, both before his wife died, he was a suspect in another unsolved rape but the victim didn't show in court, case dropped...

"Stop," Lewis said. "Just print it all out. We can't remember that."

"Right away," Quark responded. Papers started spewing out of the Quantum Computer into a tray. In two seconds, or so it seemed, four sheets, one sided, double spaced, lay in the tray.

"Quark, print two extra copies of each page."

Eight sheets fell into the tray in two seconds flat. Clark gathered them up, put them in order and gave one to Baer, Smithe, and copies for Lewis and himself.

Jake took his copies and sat in the closest chair to him and read. Smithe stood and went through his. Meriwether Lewis and William Clark laid theirs aside on Clark's desk for later study. Everyone was silent as Baer and Smithe read.

Speaking first after reading the complete report, Baer said, "I can check this Zabinski guy out tomorrow. Should be easy. But in this business, nothing is easy."

"You got that right," Smithe said.

"Who's funding this operation?"

"The victim's husband, don't know his name—wishes to remain anonymous. He's one thoroughly, angry, pissed off, guy though."

Frowning Baer said, "That makes two of us. I can't promise I'll string 'em up by the balls but they'll know they are about to die and why. Guaranteed."

Smithe unwrapped a stick of chewing gum, stuck it into his mouth and said, "That's what he really means."

"What about his wife?"

"She wants no part of it. As a matter of fact, she doesn't want to know anything and can't remember anything. She also won't cooperate even if she does remember…so she says. She knows nothing about his contract with us."

Stretching his legs out Jake said, "What's her problem? Doesn't she want justice?"

"Her *problem,* as you put it, is that she wants to forget it, not forgive them or to punish them but to forget the whole event."

"I've got news for her. She will never forget what happened to her, maybe forget details but not the raping. She needs therapy help." Baer put his hands behind his head.

Chewing, smacking, cracking the gum John Smithe spit it into a trash can. "I want to go back to smoking. This shit pisses me off."

"Chewing gum?"

"No! These damn men or boys who think they can do this and get away with it."

"What's up with the girl, uh, woman who got raped? Does she finally want to do something about it?" Lewis asked.

"Like I just told Jake, my understanding is that she is still not cooperating very well. Brings back bad memories," Smithe said. "And like I said she doesn't know about us. Neither does the victim's husband.

"Well ain't that too damn bad," Clark said. "It brings back bad memories. Well do something about it woman."

Fuming Lewis added, "No justice, no peace."

Baer said, "I'm going back to my house, think, work up some plans, and be back here when I have something. Then I'll tell you geek brothers what I want done."

"We're not brothers," Clark specified. "Our bothers are at NSA; we've told you before. By the way, who will you be this time, Winston Smart again?"

Baer grinned at them. "I'll be no name and any name that I happen to think of. Don't want to stick with one name this time."

"Neither do we," Lewis said.

Clark chuckled.

Baer stood and so did the senator. They didn't speak as they left the "Underground."

Lewis and Clark said nary a word. Not even a good-bye, since they were pissed at the victim. They tried not to be too involved except to dispense info and fly the surplus Predator drone, that was always waiting at the Clinton-Sherman Airport in Oklahoma.

They also had three smaller drones behind the senator's house, housed in one medium shed. They helped the Oklahoma police in high-speed chases. Each carried a mini-gun—just in case. They gave the Oklahoma Highway Patrol the idea and furnished the first pair for them. Better than a helicopter and they were "invisible".

Smithe was not in a frame of mind to give the Maryland or Virginia police any information they had about the drones. He didn't trust them. So he kept them ready for his people to use.

8

Baer drove home and settled in an easy chair with a beer. He went through the stapled print-out from Quark. So far Quark was only able to identify one perp and one dead witness. One still lived in Dundalk and the others—were—where? He read only Zabinski's dossier, not the history that went with it, that was on another sheet.

Dossier:	Clint Zabinski. Intel date, Aug., 2020
Born:	August 12, 1948
Place:	St. Joseph's Hospital, Baltimore, MD.
Childhood Home:	1905 Steelship Rd., Dundalk, MD. 21222
Graduated:	Dundalk Sr. High, 1966
Nickname:	Flint, from movie, In Like Flint
Employment:	Bethlehem Steel, Sparrow's Point, MD. retired early because of injury, left hand crushed.
Married:	1975 Fathered one boy and two girls. Names not important. Children live away from home.

Widowed:	2015
Remarried:	No. Woman, Gloria Steinberg, lives there as common law. 2017.
Children:	All have long criminal records.
Domicile:	24 Barford Ave., Dundalk, MD. 21222
Land Line:	none
Cell:	unknown, possible burner.
Criminal Record(s):	Two citations for disorderly conduct. Both before wife died. Police suspected he might have killed wife but no proof. Suspected of rape but the victim was a no show in court. Case dismissed.
Service Record(s)	none
END	

He took a pull of his beer, thinking. *I'm going to have to find the girl/ woman, who had the party. I need to get all of the info at one time. Hopefully, at least, all of their names.*

After a minute he decided on the farthest first. Less of a distraction locally. He got up and went to his laptop on the desk. He lifted the lid and booted it. He typed in Google maps. *How convenient to spy on someone's location.* He took another swig of beer. Baer studied the aerial view of Scott Turner's Florida house. His development looked like an old wagon wheel. Then he went to the street view.

Baer thought that he could rent a car and drive down. After the deed, fly back. Last, he felt now, would be Dundalk. So Kenneth Black was picked next since he lived in Essex, MD.

Yet Baer knew things would be fluid but he still needed to make some kind of plans. Betty continued her stonewalling—refusing to remember who they were. He still couldn't understand the mindset of Elizabeth. Strange that she didn't want justice, even if it opened old wounds. He thought it would be worth the pain. He would guarantee it. In this day and age of so-called equality, the minds of women were always different than men.

Little did he know that his mind and plans would be changing soon.

Clint Zabinski sat at the bar in the Stevedore's Tavern located on Dundalk Avenue in Dundalk. It was close to his house, so he had walked there. The local watering hole brought in the colorful characters who lived in or near Dundalk. No package goods store within this establishment. Besides the bar, it contained four tables and two pool tables. Sometimes Zabinski would shoot some pool with other locals that he knew. He got to know quite a few since he had to retire early from getting his left hand smashed at the Point. His hand worked fine for him except that he couldn't hold heavy items like a hammer. A beer mug he could hold if he held it a certain way. The way he held it made newcomers look. The regulars didn't pay any attention. Lucky for him he held a cue stick just fine since he was right-handed. The damaged left hand became a benefit. The cue stick fit in a damaged groove nicely. He would play for money and mostly beat everyone. Then he'd get cocky and make himself a nuisance.

Tonight, no games. He had an argument with his live-in woman over one of his delinquent kids, usually over Tammi, one of his two girls. She wanted some money for her drug habit and Clint was about to give it to her when his woman stepped in. Yapping about that was wasting money, going down the toilet, we need food, same old shit, he thought. That was why he was here tonight—giving his money to the bartender.

"Looks like you need another beer, Flint," the bartender said.

"Maybe in a bit." Clint looked around, a slow night. No one at the pool tables. Good, he wasn't in the mood anyway. Two guys sat at a table, drinking and talking. The music was loud enough so you could talk to a person next to you but no one else could hear you.

What upset him also was that he expected a call from Scott or Jerry soon. The damn eight-month check-up for something they did over fifty-five years ago. Damn Scott couldn't let it go and he was getting damn tired of it. That bitch probably forgot long time ago all about the rape they did that night.

"Hey, Jonesy, I'll take another now."

"Here you go. Rough day at the ranch tonight?" Jonesy asked sarcastically.

Zabinski took a big gulp and set the mug down. "Yeh, same old shit and no I don't want to talk about it."

"Fine." Jonesy walked away.

After he finished the beer, he waddled out of the bar and walked home.

The next day Clint Zabinski answered his phone after two rings. Here it is. "What now, Scott?" he grunted.

"You sound as cheerful as always."

"Aw, bite me."

Scott Turner laughed. "Just keeping in touch as always. Everything cool in Dundalk?" He had been having Jerry call everyone but he decided to follow up. He needed to be sure.

"Yeah, it's always cool. Are these phone calls necessary? Man, it's been fifty-five years now. You cramp my style with these calls."

"You know Jerry or I will call everyone every eight months. We made a pact."

"Yeah, and I ain't told nobody nothing. And she don't remember."

"She might one day. You've heard of the 'MeToo' movement."

"I heard she married a big shot hick."

"Yeah, I know, but he's no hick. I'm the one who told you. Found her on *Quickie People Finder*. Like I TOLD YOU. You hitting the sauce again?"

"Just enough to wet my whistle."

"Remember, you say anything and you're gone."

"Don't threaten…" Click. "Damn, bastard—get off my back."

Zabinski thought, Scott and this Corona Virus bull shit was always bothering him. Damn State's still checking on people too.

Zabinski called Jesse Delaney. "Yeah," answered a drunken voice.

"This is Clint. Did Scott call you?"

Slurring his words, he said, "Ah, yeh, this morning. That's why I'm celebrating with a drink." Jesse had a landline and no answering machine.

"Lay off the booze Jesse, before you shoot off your mouth and get us in trouble. Scott's doing his eight-month re-checking."

"I ain't gonna get no ones in trouble. Soon I'm a gonna head to Lil Itlee and get a nice young thing." He heard a click. "Still a hothead," Jesse said to the phone.

Turner called Jerry Gannon and Kenny Black. Jerry said that he had already called everyone last month. No need to check on him. Told Turner to relax. Jerry didn't rile easy but if you pissed him off, he'd buck up.

Next was Black, same type of call but a little more push back from Black. Black told him to quit checking on him. He didn't rape her. Scott Turner didn't trust any of them. He was successful and respected and he wanted to make sure it stayed that way. He lived in South West Florida, the good life, and no one would take him down. *Damn this guilt feeling after all these years. Damn MeToo.*

"You know why I make these calls."

"Sounds like a personal problem to me," Black said. "So quit bugging me."

"Yeah, it'll be your problem if you open your trap."

"What got you all riled up?" Black had more spunk in him than the others, except for Scott.

"That alky, Jesse is drunk and one day he's gonna slip up but I think I can fix that."

"I don't wanna hear any more."

"You're going to hear more. Because if he screws up, we'll all go down. So I'll be looking for an eraser."

"Ah shit, Scott, now you're gonna get me involved in a murder." He wasn't in for that kind of spunk.

"Just remember what I said."

Black jumped when he heard the phone slam down. Scott was using an old land line also and it had a temper.

For the first time in fifty-five years, Black was worried. What the hell happened to get Turner worked up? He didn't know what he should do. He had no place to go and no money to run. Maybe he could live with his sister in Halfway, Maryland. The city got its name for being halfway between Hagerstown and Williamsport.

He'd try. Black speed dialed her number.

"Hello," a sweet voice greeted.

"Hi, sis, it's me."

"What the hell do you want? Money?"

He noticed the animosity in her tone. Evidently, she also used an old phone with no caller I.D. What's wrong with her and Scott?

"I didn't call to fight or wanting money. I called…"

"You want something, I bet," she interrupted.

Black forced himself to stay calm. "I called because I need a favor."

"Humph. I knew it."

"Can I stay at your house for a few days while mine is being remodeled," he lied.

"When?"

"Sometime this week."

"Yeah, I guess. But I want the yard mowed and my shutters painted." She spit out the last sentence.

Man, she made him mad. "Be glad to do it. Thanks, sis." He hoped it sounded sarcastic.

She hung up. At least she didn't slam it.

9

Baer decided the best way to go about this is to find old classmates who would know Abigail Beecher. He posed as a husband of a dead alumni and joined both Dundalk Alumni groups. He thought he had a hit with Mary Higgins but she didn't know Abigail's married name. The woman thought Abby had married twice. She had seen her in Dundalk a few times a couple of years ago but didn't talk with her any length of time. Baer checked the Quickie People Finder site for her two known brothers. No Abigail was listed as a relation or possible relation. He'd have to let Quark and the geeks dig deeper—and he assumed they were doing just that. He decided to go with Clint Zabinski. Found him still living in Dundalk, he had the wife who died three years ago. Now he had a common law relationship with his new woman. The three children, one boy and two girls, from his marriage, were living their own reckless lives elsewhere in Baltimore County and Baltimore City.

Zabinski had three disorderly conduct criminal records since 2011. All three of his children, the son and two daughters, had disorderly conduct charges against them. Most were for assaults with fists or knives, illegal drugs, mostly marijuana, and traffic—speeding and causing wrecks. The girls seemed the worst of the siblings. Another happy family.

The Dossier was right.

Baer didn't care about the grown kids, unless they got in the way. His focus was on daddy Clint. Before he could kill Clint, he'd like to get even a little info out of him about the others.

Baer decided he'd pose as a health care worker checking the county paperwork for Covid-19. He'd get the fake documents from the computer sleuths. Time to pay a visit to Clint since he can't find Abigail Beecher. He smiled to himself. *I wonder if she was a history teacher?*

Baer drove a rented dull silver Toyota SUV and parked it down and across the street from Zabinski's white cape cod styled house with fake shutters. Neat and clean yard with nick-knacks under the front window. The house had "a woman lives here" look. Baer faced the SUV in the opposite direction so when he left, he would be driving away from the house. He glanced at his watch: 1:38 P.M.

The Dundalk neighborhood was old but very well kept up by the citizens. They were proud of their enclave and it showed. Houses were close but everything had an air of privacy. Baer felt good about this.

Baer gathered his clipboard with its pen hanging from it. He wore a black wig with a man bun. He checked himself in the mirror and the phony scar across his forehead still looked good, so did his brown contacts and his tan from a bottle. He placed a pair of black frame glasses on his face. Then he felt for his Smith and Wesson 918, 9mm in his white sport coat pocket. The other pocket held the silencer. Placing his Covid mask around his neck he fixed it in place on his face, opened the car door and exited. Baer strolled diagonally to Zabinski's house. His all white attire and glasses made him look like a medical professional. This neighborhood had seen a lot of doctor and nurse types canvassing the area on occasion. He blended in with the policy to make sure Covid-19 wouldn't start up again. The governor demanded that health professionals keep tabs on the people. The Chevy in the driveway let him know someone was home. Plenty of trees lined the street in the neighborhood and shrubs that would block some nosy people, if any were watching. He reached the door and rang the bell.

The door opened and an old looking Zabinski stood there looking perturbed.

"Now what? When are you guys going to stop this?"

"I'm sorry but we have to do this. Got to stay safe and healthy. Your neighbors are going through this also. The state knows best."

"Bull shit. I don't care. I don't like it." He stepped aside and let Baer in. "Damn government."

"This won't take long. Is your wife home?"

"Nah. She's at the mall. I'm here all by my damn self. Whada you need?"

"First would you get your papers from the last Medical visit?" Maryland had become a police state. The people buckled easily. Except for a few die hards.

"Wait here." Zabinski walked down a short hall and went into a room.

Baer had checked everything earlier, no dogs, no kids, now no wife in the house. The jerk had the disorderly conduct attitude. Perfect. Baer laid his clipboard down, reached into both pockets and retrieved the gun and silencer and put them together. He took the safety off and stretched his arms in a two-handed grip. Zabinski came back and his eyes bugged.

"What the hell!"

"Stand perfectly still, Clint. I have a message for you." Baer could see a wet spot forming around his crotch. He had that effect on people—when he had a gun aimed at them. Zabinski stood there shaking hard enough for the papers he was holding to flap a little. Clint's brain and motor skills were in the third choice. Freeze. Fight or flight was not an option.

"You did something criminal back in mid nineteen sixty-five. Remember the name Elizabeth or Betty?"

"Ah, I can't think now. What do you want?"

Baer was not enjoying this. "Remember her?!"

"Ah, yes." He shook more. "I'm sorry. How did you know?"

"Know what, shit-head? That you and your gang raped her?"

"I'm sorry." He started to blubber. "We were kids having fun."

"Fun!" Baer screamed at him. *Cool it man.* Baer spoke softly, "You ruined her life and that of her husband."

Clint started to cry now. "Scott said this might happen. Just don't kill me. I'll make it up to her." Now he whimpered.

Great. The shithead told me a name. "Tell me Scott's last name and the names of the others and I might let you go."

"Uh, I can't think."

"Scott's last name. Think quickly, asshole, or I'll kill you now," Baer said.

"Scott Turner, he was the ringleader," he said, still shaking.

"The others. I don't want to pry it out of you."

"Uh, Kenny Black. I can't think of the others. You're scaring me." Tears were running down his cheeks. "I'll make it up to her. Please."

"Too late for that shithead. Her husband wants you strung up by the balls, but that's not my style."

Standing there shaking, eyeing the gun, and crying he pleaded, "Don't kill me."

Baer smiled as he noticed the wet spot grew ever larger.

"Remember anyone else?"

"No. I can't think. Please."

"Give me another name!"

"I, I can't think!" Zabinski shook violently but had stopped crying.

"For Elizabeth." Baer fired one shot into his forehead, between the eyes.

Clint Zabinski was dead before he hit the floor. Baer looked at him stretched out with his ankles crossed and said, "One shithead gone." Looking at him, he shrugged his shoulders. "No need for more questions. You pled guilty." Next time he'd have to control his disgust, for he thought about putting more bullets into him. That wouldn't be professional.

Baer disassembled the weapon and put the parts back into his coat pockets. *Get out before the woman comes home.* Then he went to the door and peeked out and saw nothing unusual. He grabbed his clipboard and opened the door. He locked it from the inside. Again, he put his mask up, covering his face. He strode back to his car looking at his clipboard, pretending to write something important. When he reached the car and got in, he threw the clipboard on the seat, pulled off his rubber gloves and threw them on the floor. Starting the car, he slowly left. He reached Liberty Parkway, turned left onto it and found a spot to park. He pulled off the mask and called Smithe on his cell phone using code.

"Go," answered Smithe.

"Hit a home run, with three on base, one on deck, going to the lockers." Baer's baseball code told Smithe that Clint Zabinski was eliminated, four more predators to kill, and that he would be arriving at the ex-senator's house as soon as possible.

"See you then."

They disconnected. Baer took the chip and the battery out of the phone. He then eased out onto Liberty Parkway and headed back to Smithe's.

Clint's live-in significant other, Gloria, came home an hour later and parked her Toyota Camry, blocking the Chevy. At the door she put her packages down and unlocked the door. No one ever had their doors unlocked so it was automatic for her to do. As soon as she stepped inside, she screamed.

The first white Ford Police Interceptor SUV arrived within three minutes after she called. Officer Kelly fixed his ball cap and heard loud wailing. He ran through the open door into the house and stopped short. A sobbing woman was cradling a man's head in her arms. He went up to her and tried to gently pull her away.

"Ma'am, I'm sorry. Please let go."

"He's dead! Someone killed him!" She wailed.

Soft and gentle didn't work.

"Ma'am let go!" He pried her arms from him and she slipped back to hold her man. He tried again, slipping and tugging, only to dragged her and Clint across the floor a foot. He let go. He looked at himself—shirt full of blood.

"Shit, the scene is already contaminated." From his lapel mic, he called for backup, and a detective—and the county forensic investigators.

Two new Ford Interceptor SUVs arrived in two minutes with lights and sirens. The detective arrived seven minutes later. Looking at the uniform he asked the officer initially on the scene. "What have we got?"

"A fucking mess."

"I see that by your uniform. Whad you do, wrestle with the deceased?"

"Yeah, and the woman. Far as I can tell the male vic was shot once in the face at close range."

Detective John Bullock raised his eyebrows, then squatted and looked at the papers near the body. He thought out loud. "Looks like Covid-19 reports. Wonder why he had those?"

The detective looked at two of the officers. "Start knocking on doors and see if anyone heard or saw anything."

"Okay." They left.

Before the last uniform left, Kelly said, "Before I tried to pry her off of him and messed up the body position, I did notice, his ankles were crossed."

"Hmm. Dead man's fall."

"What's that?"

"He might have known the killer or the killer surprised him at the last second. As the vic stood or moved towards the killer, he got shot, and he was dead instantly before he hit the floor."

"Damn."

The detective thought, good to know that piece of info.

Later that day at his office Bullock got the written reports from forensics. One fatal shot to the frontal head area. No other injuries. No prints, other than family. Nothing missing. The Common Law wife, Gloria, unlocked the door. All other doors and windows locked. No forced entry. No security cameras. The canvassing officers found that no one saw or heard anything. Earlier Bullock had called forensics for details on the bullet, etc. Forensics said he'd call back when he finished the examination.

The detective thought, *if I didn't know better, I'd say this was a contract killing.* "Shit, I'll never find him."

Bullock typed into his computer. "I better check Zabinski's background."

He found that Clint had three felonies—but ran into a dead end as he expected. Nothing stood out to warrant the murder. *This damn case is gonna go cold. I'll have to find his friends, if he had any.*

Forensics called on his iPhone. "Yeah?"

"I'd say, close range, one bullet, nine mil., probably a black talon, judging by the damage in the middle of the forehead, between the eyes. Brain totally destroyed. Never saw it coming."

"Thanks." He disconnected. *I was right, he saw it coming, doc, dead before he hit the floor. Contract killing. Why? What made him so important?* He got up and went to the coffee machine. Brought the coffee back to his desk and wrote up the report with his comments.

10

Baer walked to the side entrance of John Smithe's house and rang the bell. The senator had plenty of greenery blocking the view. Jeeves answered the door.

"Come in, sir."

"How's it going Jeeves?"

"Very well, sir. The senator will meet you in the library. This way, sir."

Baer followed without saying another word. He knew where the library was. Jeeves was just doing his job.

"Have a seat, sir. The senator will be with you momentarily."

"Thanks, Jeeves."

Baer picked a chair to wait.

"Jake, my boy." Smithe patted him on the shoulder as he went by and picked a chair close to him. "Got some good news."

"You're getting married," Baer blurted out.

Smithe ignored him. "Quark found Abigail Beecher under her second husband's name—Jones. But she's living with a guy named Swann. I'll give you the paperwork before you leave. You go see her and be your friendly, suave self, to get the other predator's names. We might need a letter from Betty Kephart to get you in the door. But that would be a problem. Then

Betty would know somethings up. We're not supposed to know that we know who's funding this. But thanks to Quark, we know."

"She doesn't know a thing, and that's the way her husband wants it." Baer clasped his hands in front of his stomach.

"You're right. We'll forget that—that's where your charm comes in."

Baer rolled his eyes. "Do I play doctor again with the next one?"

"You know better. New disguise, new bull crap each time."

"Just wanted to see if you had something different in mind."

"You might be an electrician or water department. We'll see when the time comes." *Quark would decide the best way.* Smithe rang a bell on the side table by his chair.

Jeeves appeared almost instantly. "You rang," he said in a deep voice.

Baer snickered. Reminded him of Lurch.

"Bring us a glass of Cognac, please."

"Very good, sir."

Baer smiled, then turned serious. "If they all still live in Dundalk, the jobs will be tricky and have to be spaced out and carefully planned. If they live far apart, the jobs will still have to be very well planned, but can be one after the other."

"Yes, but things can still get disrupted."

Jeeves arrived with the drinks, served them and left.

Bear took a sip. "So, I'll use my own discretion in talking to Abby Jones or Swann, or whatever name she's using."

"Whichever she chooses, of course. You have carte blanche. I don't know her but you will. All she has to tell you is their names. If she asks you anything tell her what you think fits. Just don't tell her the truth."

"Come on, John—I know what to say."

"I know, I know. Sorry. It's crimes like these guys pulled off that keep me pissed off."

"Are all the drones ready?"

"Yes. Any or all that you need to use."

"Including Mighty Midget?"

"Yes."

Mighty Midget is their nickname of the drone officially called Killer Looking, with four props, double blades. Its' machine gun holds 1000 rounds, and state of the art high def cameras—in a small package. Range: 100 miles. Top speed: 100 miles per hour. Flying time: 1½ hrs.

They finished their drinks and Smithe called downstairs to the Underground to have Clark bring up the paperwork on Abigail Swann. Clark was up in a flash and handed it to Baer.

"Thanks, Clark." Baer said.

"Just doing my job while you all drink your night caps early."

"You get paid plenty," snorted Smithe.

"And worth every penny. Good night." Clark strolled away chuckling.

11

When Baer got home, he fixed his dinner of spaghetti and meat sauce with red onions mixed in. While the spaghetti was boiling, he went to the fridge and reached for a bottle of *Our Daily Red* natural wine, no added sulfites. He poured himself a glass and sat at the dining room table, where the dossier on Abagail Swann laid waiting. He opened the manila folder and pulled out the single page dossier. The paper gave the basics and he skimmed through it. She lived in Middle River with her 67-year-old "husband" Thomas Swann. Her age was listed at 71. Jake smiled. *Went younger the third time around.* First husband, Roger Smith died in an auto crash. His eyes went back up to the top of the page.

Dossier:	Abigail J. Swann. Intel date, Sept. 2020
Abagail Swann, nee:	Beecher, married Smith; married Jones
Born:	June 7, 1949 age 71
Place:	Baltimore, MD. Cities Hospital
Childhood Home:	Dundalk, MD.
Graduated:	Dundalk Senior High School, 1967
Nickname:	Abby

Employments:	Baltimore Life Ins. Co.; Bundle and Cook Law Offices; Style Wright Beauty Solon, Owner Barbara Wright—last known employer.
Married:	1st husband, Roger Smith June 21, 1970
Born:	July 7, 1948
	No children
Widowed:	January 5, 1998, auto crash

☼

Married:	2nd husband, Kyle Jones August 16, 2001. Husband age 72
Born:	Oct. 1,1948
	No children
Divorced:	Sept 11, 2003
	Ex-husband of Kandla Jones, a co-worker at the beauty shop.

☼

Married:	common law, 2004, 3rd "husband" Thomas Swann, age 67.
Profession:	retired Conklin Ford salesman, Middle River, MD.
Born:	Dec. 2, 1953
Domicile:	1111 Hardwood Rd., Middle River, MD.
Land Line:	410-555-1459
Cell:	443-555-2068
Service Record(s):	Army, 2 yrs., Vietnam
END	

Happy hunting Jake, the Geeks

Baer rubbed his chin and looked at his Tiffany watch. Too late to call and his spaghetti noodles were boiling over. He jumped up and took the pot off the burner. He saved it just in time. He finished preparing his dinner and brought it to the table. He ate, thought, and looked over the dossier. The more he thought about it, he decided the direct approach would be the best—with a few embellishments.

He finished his meal and put the dirty dishes into the dishwasher. Then he went for the wine bottle and poured another glass and took it over to the chair where the scramble phone was. He dialed Abby's number. A man answered. "Hello."

"Hi. This is Rick Moore. I'm a member of the Dundalk Alumni Association and I'm looking for a former classmate, Abigail Beecher, who I understand is Abigail Jones. Is this the right number?"

"Yes. I'm her husband, Tom Swann. You said you were her classmate?"

"Yes, but a different graduating class, twenty-oh-two. We are trying to get in touch with everyone to make a special updated memoir book. May I be able to speak with her?"

"Sure. I think she'd be happy to hear from someone from Dundalk High. Hold on."

About thirty seconds later, a woman's voice. "Hello?" Caution in her tone.

"Hi Abigail. This is Rick Moore and I'm with the Dundalk Alumni and we're trying to contact as many of the alumni as we can for a special memorial book."

"Yes, Tom told me."

"I was wondering if I could speak with you in person, take notes and maybe borrow a photo, if you are willing. It would mean an awful lot to everyone."

There was a ten second pause.

"Uh, I guess so. Yeah, that would be cool. Do you have my address?"

"No," he lied. "But I'm ready to write it down."

As she gave him the address, he sipped his wine while looking at the dossier to make sure it was right. It was.

"Where do you live?" Abigail asked with enthusiasm.

"Rockville," he said.

"Well, that's not too far."

"Nope. How does tomorrow at ten a.m. look?"

"Well, one-thirty would be better."

"Not a problem. I'll see you tomorrow at one-thirty."

"Okay. Thanks for calling."

"My pleasure. Bye."

Baer smiled and took the last of his wine. *In like Flint.*

Baer called Smithe. "A meeting with Abigail Jones has been accomplished."

"I knew you could do it," Smithe answered. "When?"

"Tomorrow, one-thirty, her house."

"Wearing a disguise, right?"

"Lightly. Brown wig, brown contacts and a brown mole."

"Isn't the mole extreme?"

"Nothing is extreme in this business. She'll remember the mole more than anything."

"I see. Good luck." Smithe hung up.

Baer arrived at Abigail's house promptly at one-thirty. The Mister wasn't with her. They made the usual pleasantries, then Baer got right to business.

"Abigail, the purpose…"

"Oh, call me Abby. Everyone does."

Baer smiled. "Okay, Abby. The reason I'm here is to collect the names of some classmates I think you might know."

"Oh, well, I have my yearbooks on the dining room table. Let's go there."

"Great."

They walked over and Abby said, "Would you like some coffee or tea?"

"Coffee would be fine, but don't go to any trouble."

"No trouble. It's instant."

Baer cringed inside. "If you don't mind." This was going smoother than he thought it would, even though the instant coffee was going to be rough. Anything to keep her happy.

She delivered the coffee, nuked no less. Baer took a courtesy sip. "Thank you."

They settled down at the table with the Year Books. She had all of her three years. At that time, 1967, Dundalk Senor High had only 3 grades: sophomore, junior, senior.

He laid his mid-sized notebook on the table with the names he knew. He read the first one. "Clint Zabinski." He waited for her reaction.

She jumped slightly. "Yes. I know him. I saw on TV that he was murdered a few days ago." She mumbled something.

"What was that? I didn't hear." Baer leaned forward.

"Let's just say he wasn't on my list of people I liked or wanted to associate with."

Baer noticed she fidgeted slightly. Good.

"Why is that?"

"He was a creep and still is…or was. Good riddance to bad rubbish." Her voice had a bite.

"Would you tell me why you feel that way?"

"He's dead. Let him enjoy where he is."

"Where would that be, Abby?"

"Hell, I hope." She covered her mouth. "I shouldn't have said that."

He thought he'd take a chance. "Abby, I'm gonna level with you. I'm working privately on a cold case and I really need your help. Did you have a party at your parent's house around September, nineteen sixty-five? And was Clint at the party?"

"Do I need a lawyer?"

Baer put on his best smile and calming voice. "No, nothing like that. I'm just gathering information. This is and will be strictly confidential between you and me."

"Can I have my husband here?"

Baer was expecting that but hoped it wouldn't come to it. "Yes, of course, if that will make you feel more comfortable."

"He's outside pulling weeds." She went to get him.

Two minutes went by and she came back with Thomas Swann, smiling, trying to look sharp with his wrap around hairstyle, bald on top.

"I hear you're a private eye," Thomas said as they shook hands. He had cleaned them.

A good sign, thought Baer. "Oh no sir," Baer smiled. "I told Abby I was working privately on a cold case."

"Officially?"

"No, a hobby really. A friend knew I was going to be in Baltimore so she asked me to check."

"Check on what?"

"To see if I could find the names of certain men who were at Abby's party in nineteen sixty-five. She couldn't remember the names. She said that Abby would help me."

Tom sat back. "Who's the she?"

Baer looked at him seriously. "That's confidential at this point, sir. Just like what is said here today is confidential."

Tom rubbed his chin. "Is this necessary?"

With a hard look Baer said, "Very."

"Can I end this at any time."

"Yes, but you will not want to."

Tom folded his hands in front of him, twisting them. "If it doesn't get Abby into any trouble…then go ahead."

"I guarantee, Abby will not get into trouble. As a matter of fact, there probably will be great rejoicing. So, let's get started again. Abby, was Clint at the party?"

"Yes, he was."

Do you remember all of the boys, men now, at the party?"

"Yes."

"Okay. Who else?" *Here we go.*

"Kenny Black."

"Kenneth Black?"

"Yes."

"If you can remember their full names. Please." Baer wrote.

"Kenneth Black was at the party but didn't go with the others and Betty."

"Do you know why?"

"My guess would be that the car was full. It had bucket seats. That Jesse had a good-looking car and…"

"I'm sorry, Abby. Just the names, please." *Women, and their overabundance of unnecessary details.* He was on a hot streak and wanted to keep it going.

"Scott Turner. Jerry Gannon. Jesse, somebody, I don't know his last name. He bought the alcohol. I heard at a class reunion a few years ago that Jesse had an auto wreck but he lived. Wasn't hurt too bad."

Baer wrote as fast as she talked. "I'm really sorry to hear that," he said facetiously.

"Yeah. He was a dumb jerk. Those are the ones Betty left the party with."

"Jerry Gannon. Was Gerald his full name?"

"I don't know. I only knew him as Jerry. Never heard anybody call him Gerald. He's in the yearbook. Let's see." She started flipping pages and stopped when she spotted her photo. "This is me."

Tom went over to take a look. "My, you sure were pretty." Then quickly he said, "and you are still."

"Thanks, you big liar."

Even Baer looked at her picture, then looked at her. *Damn, more wrinkles than an un-ironed shirt. Short curly pink highlighted hair and probably a hundred and fifty pounds heavier.*

She flipped a couple more pages and stopped when she found Gannon's photo. "Here he is."

"Can I take a photo of him?"

"Sure. You can take photos of all that are in the book."

Baer took his iPhone and snapped Jerry's picture. She turned the pages until she found Turner. Baer snapped a shot. Then she went to the beginning and found Black—Baer got him too.

"You want to see what Clint looked like in high school?"

"I'll pass." *He's dead, woman.* Suddenly he changed his mind. The client might want it. "Yes, let me get his picture." He snapped it. "Do you know where any of them might be now."

"I hope Hell. That's probably where I'll go since I didn't stop her. I don't know where any of the creeps are."

"What did you do after she left?"

"I called Freddy Ragsdale."

"Not the cops?" he emphasized.

She looked down. "No," she whispered. Her concerned "husband" put his hand over hers. In a low sad tone, she continued, "Anyway, Freddie's dead. He turned into a jerk, also. He had women live with him or he lived with them. Whatever. I should have stopped her."

Noticing her heartbreak, plus he had enough to go on, Baer calmly said, "Thank you. You've been very helpful."

"No, I haven't. I should have done something." Tears streamed down her cheeks. "I should have told the police back then."

Baer wanted to convince her, "Abby, you have been a *tremendous* help. I can assure you. And I guarantee they *will* face justice."

"Will she have to testify or anything?" Tom asked.

"No. No she won't. That's a guarantee," Baer said as he looked Tom straight in the eye.

Tom closed his eyes for a couple of seconds. He was savvy enough to know what that meant. When he opened them, he had the look of fear. *Oh shit.* Looking into those cold, lifeless brown contacts, he knew a killer when he saw one.

Abigail turned to her "husband", they embraced and she cried. "I'm so sorry."

Baer got up and nodded to her husband, "Thank you." With moist eyes, Tom nodded back. Baer walked out of the house.

12

As Baer drove back to Smithe's house he wondered why Elizabeth didn't want to pursue justice against these men. They got away with it for over fifty-five years, raping an unwilling sixteen-year-old girl. Be that as it may, the end is near for them, and Baer is bringing Hell with him.

Sitting in the senator's den, Baer handed Smithe his notes from Abby. "Got three names from her."

"By the way, Quark came up with Jesse's last name—Delaney. So, how about we go in alphabetical order?" Smithe asked.

"How about we don't. I like random."

"Okay, Jerry Gannon is next, then Scott Turner, then Kenneth Black. Delaney last."

"Sounds good." He humored Smithe.

"I'll give this to Lewis and Clark and get the dope on each one. Then off you go."

"Man, that sounds easy. No help in planning?"

"You'll get all the help you need, downstairs." He rang for Jeeves.

Quark found Jerry Gannon in Takoma Park, Maryland, off of East-West Highway on Clearview Avenue. He lived in a two-story box house number 11069. No driveway. A few home owners added driveways in that neighborhood. In the 1950s the population was all white. Now, 23% black with 8% white, with a mix of 4% Asian and a dominant 64% Hispanic. That might pose a problem, he could blend in, with disguises—he hoped. He'd still stand out like a cue ball on a billiard table. That neighborhood would be more difficult to penetrate, but not impossible.

Baer sat in Smithe's library again. He had coffee this time.

Baer sipped some, then said, "Before I go, I'll need some ideas now. I've come up with this. I'm going to have to lure him from his house to a deserted place. No go in that neighborhood. I checked it out for a prior job."

"You mean you've been there before on a job?"

"Yes, nearby, and it wasn't pretty."

Smithe waved his hand, he didn't want to know…except. "Will that prior job interfere with the present job?"

"Not sure. That's why I want to do it outside his home turf. Have Lewis and Clark work up something for me. Get me all the details of his coming and goings and the like."

"You have the dossier in your hands."

"That's basic, you know it. I need the meat. Habits, comings and goings, extra love lives, et cetera."

Smithe stroked his chin with thumb and forefinger. "I'll get a very private eye on it."

"Good." Baer slurped his coffee. "I'll go and check Gannon's neighborhood again—just in case I have to do it at his house. In the meantime, have the guys get Kenny Black and Scott Turner dossiers."

"They're already working on Turner's."

"When will they have it?"

Smithe pulled a portable phone from his pocket and pushed a button. "Lewis, when will the complete info on Scott Turner be ready?"

"Should have it in a couple of seconds. Quark is spitting the necessary papers out now."

"Bring them to the den," Smithe ordered.

"Righto."

After a few minutes of small talk between Smithe and Baer, Lewis entered the library.

"Here they are John."

"Thanks."

Lewis turned and left.

Smithe handed them to Baer. Baer scanned it.

"Looks like he did good for himself. Looks like he had a high paying job," Baer said as he laid the paper on the table. "Glancing at it I noticed he has two phone numbers. One for Florida and one for Maryland."

"Interesting," Smithe said. His intercom phone rang. He listened and said, "Bring it up."

"Lewis is bringing Black's dossier."

"Great. I think Black will be last," Baer said. He drank some coffee.

"I think we should strike at the one with the hottest iron in the fire," Smithe said.

Baer raised an eyebrow and look at John Smithe. "With all due respect and honor, John, I will decide that."

"Of course, my boy. I didn't mean it to sound like an order. It's a suggestion."

Smiling Baer said, "Suggestions will be accepted. Any other suggestions?"

"Yeah. Don't get caught."

"The order of the strikes might not be as we plan it. I can feel this will be a fluid assignment."

"Meaning?"

"Things can change suddenly."

Lewis came walking in and handed Black's dossier to Baer.

"Thanks," Baer said. "You're getting your exercise, running up and down the stairs. John you should put in some kind of a vacuum tube."

Lewis looked down at him, but ignored that remark and asked, "Do you realize that your initials are the same as some fictional characters in books and movies?"

"No, I never bothered with it."

"Jay Bee, like James Bond, Jason Bourne, Jack Bauer, and Joe Blow." Lewis walked away laughing.

"Keep walking Meriwether," Baer called after him.

With Lewis out of earshot Smithe joked, "He forgot Jim Beam."

Baer shook his head, then glanced at the paper and laid it on the table, on top of Turner's. "Lives in Essex, Maryland. I'll go for him last because of geography."

"More coffee?" Smithe asked. "Or Jim Beam?" He chortled.

"No, funny father, I'm going to hit the sack and in the morning start working on a plan for Scotty boy."

"Be careful with us old guys, we might be tough," Smithe chuckled.

"Yeah, Clint thought he was a bad ass and look what happened to him."

Still chuckling, Smithe said, "Right. Bet he was dying to leave his mistress."

"Aren't we full of humor tonight."

"Here's some more funny stuff, the cops already declared Clint Zabinski's case, cold."

"After only two weeks?"

"Quark found out that *the word* is out that they are understaffed, but the real reason is they don't care. He was a pain in their ass. Maybe they think it's better than getting the Covid. Or they could count it as a Covid death. Paperwork drops to near zero."

Baer rolled his eyes, stood and said, "See you later in the future. I'll find my way out."

"Goodnight, my boy."

13

Jake Baer's black 2019 5.0 Mustang, with heavily tinted windows, rumbled into the garage. He pushed the button to turn the engine off. Then he hit the garage door fob to close it. He entered the house and went to the kitchen, opened a drawer and dropped his car and house keys into a box inside. He headed for the bedroom, stripped his clothes off and plopped on his bed. Baer went to sleep in seconds.

One eye opened and he saw the digital clock; 7:07. Baer rose and made his way into the bathroom, connected to the bedroom. After his bathroom duties he put some sliced bacon on a frying pan. While that was frying, he whipped up a pancake mix and poured out six pancakes on a skillet. He really hated cooking, he thought as he turned the bacon over.

He carried the done food to the kitchen table and went to get the dossiers.

When he returned, he laid them out to the right side of his food. Then he poured pure Maple syrup on his bacon and pancakes. He looked at the dossiers while he ate. It was a cursory look. He studied them after his breakfast with a cup of half & half natural coffee. He concentrated on Jerry Gannon's first.

Dossier:	Gerald George Gannon. Intel date, Sept. 2020
Born:	Mar. 21,1947
Place:	Dundalk, MD. At the home, home birth.
Childhood Home:	Dundalk, MD.
Graduated:	Dundalk Senior High School, 1965
Nickname:	AKA Jerry; 3 Gs (rarely)
Employments:	Stevedore, Maryland Port Authority, fired for assault and battery on co-worker. Other employment not known, if any.
Married:	No. Multiple live-ins [prostitutes? Pimp?]
Domicile:	11069 Clearview Ave., Takoma Park, MD.
Criminal Records:	Arrested with prostitute, paid fine. Aggravated assaults, two charges.
Relatives:	other siblings unknown (if any)
Service Record(s):	none
Extra intel:	Gannon's House between Takoma Landing Apts. and another group of apts. Maybe good site to fly the drone from.
END	

With the coffee cup emptied he got up to get some more. He poured the last of it into his tall black ceramic cup with the Canadian County, Oklahoma sheriff's logo on one side. A gift from Lance Pruitt. He picked up Scott Turner's next and scanned through it.

Dossier:	Scott (N.M.I.) Turner. Intel date, Oct. 2020
Born:	Apr. 15, 1949
Place:	St. Joseph's Hospital, Baltimore, MD.
Childhood Home:	Dundalk, MD.
Graduated:	Dundalk Senior High, 1967
Nickname:	None
Employment(s):	Bethlehem Steel, Sparrows Point, retired (when the plant closed) supervisor manager for coke mill. Kept supervisors' job, after coke mill was shut down in 1991 and laid off 400 workers.
Married:	Claudia VanWinkle, age 65; on June 6, 1973; he 24, she 18.
Born:	Sept. 2, 1955
Widowed:	No
Domicile:	4425 Rotary Circle, Rotonda West, FL.
Land Line:	540-555-1492
Cell:	443-555- 1560 (Maryland code)
Facebook:	Yes
Criminal Record:	Arrested for rape. Charge was dropped when victim changed her story.
Religion:	"Born again" Christian in 1977
Church:	Rotonda Lutheran Church of Fellowship. Church close by. Pastor is Rickie Tickie, small time hood and con artist. Real Name, George Pepper.

Can get Dossier on him if needed.

Service Record(s):	none
	Quark found S. Turner had sex with his wife's younger sister, age 15 at the time…house sitter, when they went on vacation.
END	

He'll tell the geeks not to bother with Rickie Tickie. He's not on the contract. He'll check Scott out first. He might have raped again. He'll have to kill him even if his conversion's real. He might talk to the pastor first, even though he's also a criminal. Get more info on Scott, make him talk or threaten to expose him to his congregation and the police. Don't need a dossier for that. A good bluff works well. So, ol' Scott raped two underage girls in his life, that we know of. The job was to kill only the rapists, but not the people around the targets—unless they got in the way.

Sipping his coffee, he reached for Black's dossier.

Dossier:	Kenneth Earl Black. Intel date, Sept. 2020
Born:	July 28, 1948
Place:	Baltimore, MD. Cities Hospital
Childhood Home:	Dundalk, MD.
Graduated:	Dundalk Sr. High School, 1966
Nickname:	AKA Duke, like the song "Duke of Earl"
Employments:	High's Dairy Store, 1967; SS Kresge, 1973; Esso/Exxon gas station, 1978; Wishy Washy Window Cleaning Co., 1988-1998; Did not mention his criminal records with employers, when they found out he was fired; unemployed (welfare) since 1999.

Married:	Jennifer Cooper, Oct. 12, 1970; no children
Divorced:	March 1977
Domicile:	4111 Black Eyed Susan Ave., Essex, MD.
	Small cape cod, 2 single front windows, door in middle. Grandparents gave to him after their deaths. Houses close together. Chain link fence around property. Dead end road. Acre of woods at dead end.
Land Line:	none
Cell:	Known to use "burners".
Criminal Record(s):	Arrested for lewd action with minor; arrested for indecent exposure; arrested for attempted rape, case dismissed, victim wasn't positive; aggravated assault; citation for being around minor girls; Jail time, 1-3 yrs.; other punishments, fines—$100 to $1000.
Religion:	Himself [none]
Service Record(s):	none
END	

"This son-of-bitch is definitely dead," he said aloud. He finished off the coffee. "I think I'll visit him next after all. This one needs to go. The others can wait."

After his late breakfast, lunch really, Baer left his house and drove to McLean, VA. to get on I-495N and followed that to I-95N. Around 50 minutes later he took exit 59 from I-95N to MD. 150, which was the E/

Eastern Ave. exit and drove into Essex, MD. Took him one hour and ten minutes one way with tolls that he paid with E-Z Pass, including fake I D, from the underground. To while away the time, he played a variety of music on his thumb drive. Songs from the 60s to the 80s mostly. Getting close to his destination he switched the music to *Fall Out Boy* to pump him up.

He had decided to drive the 5.0 Mustang for this reconnoiter and mission. He reached 4111 Black Eyed Susan Ave. at 2:47 P.M. and proceeded to drive down the short road to the dead-end videoing everything. He spotted a rundown house for sale and snapped a picture of the Real Estate sign. He reached the dead end and backed the car into the house across the street from Black's. It looked similar to the one that was for sale, only in slightly better shape. Baer sat there for five seconds while the dash cam kept recording, then he pulled slowly away and left the area. He came to Eastern Avenue and made a right and when he came to an art gallery store that was behind Black's house. He pulled in and parked in the last space on the right of the store. It faced to the right of Black's house but the house couldn't be seen because of one small and two large trees. *This is good,* he thought. *Just a sagging chain link fence, easy to get over and it wasn't blocking entrance to the mini woods.* Baer was facing the back of the neighbor's house. There wasn't a fence around the neighbor's house. Its back was blocked by a large tree in the back yard also, close to the alley. So it was not a major concern.

Baer's Ford Mustang had 20% tint on the side windows and the back. The darkness of his tint was illegal in Maryland and Virginia so he had the Oklahoma plates on the car and the papers in the glove box. He also had his Oklahoma driver's license. The 20% tinted windows blocked any prying eyes as he put on a black/brown long curly hair wig and the brown mole next to his left nostril. He always changed the position of the mole on his face. He called the mole "traveler."

He stepped out of the car, stretched, and slowly looked around. Only five vehicles in the lot with him. Good and bad, since the lot could hold five times that. Eastern Avenue was fairly busy at this time. He glanced at his watch: 3:11 P.M. He stood in front of his car, took out his small Canon digital camera, held it at his belt buckle and snapped off a few. He got back into his Mustang and looked around to see if anyone had been watching him. All clear. Started the car and rumbled out of the lot making a left, heading back to Shady Oaks.

It was getting dark when Kenny Black was walking the Eastpoint mall and watched as young girls went by. Shortly a group of giggling, bubbly, smiling, group, doing a stroll through the mall, passed him, having a good time. Black thought he'd like to have a good time with them. No dice though, too many. He kept scouting. As he passed Jimmy Jazz, he noticed a sweet young thing, about seventeen or eighteen, he guessed. Long blonde hair, tight white shorts, black T-shirt and tattoos. Girls with ink, he *knew* they were easy women. Like the theory in the old days—if she was a smoker, she'd probably go for it, sex.

He followed her as she left the Foot Locker and went into JC Penny. He went up the escalator with her, but at a discreet distance. She walked to the shoe department and he followed and came in from the opposite direction. Black pretended to look at men's shoes. When she sat down to try on a pair of Nikes, he strolled up with a box in his hand.

"That's a nice-looking pair," he said. Her tee shirt out lined her breasts perfectly.

Without looking at him she said, "Yeah."

He sat in a chair and put his box of shoes in the seat between them.

"I got to get these big clunkers. Look like corrective shoes," he chuckled.

She put her old shoes back on and put the new shoes back into the box. "I don't like these. I'm getting another pair," the girl said. She got up, went around the corner, stuck the box anywhere and quickly left without him seeing her.

Two minutes later and leaving the shoes he had picked—he rose and went to where he thought she was. Gone.

"Son-of-a bitch." He hurried to the escalator looked around, then bounded down the escalator and hurried to the exit that led outside. Looked around. Didn't see her. "Shit!" Looked like Miss Tats was street smart.

Black called it a night and went home pissed. He drove down his street to the dead end and made a U-turn to park in front of his house. He got out and slammed the door. He opened the gate and went up the two steps.

"How're you doing, Duke?" his next-door neighbor greeted while watering his flowers.

Black jerked a bit and stopped. He didn't see his neighbor, even with the porch light on. "Not good. My date stood me up."

"Sorry to hear that. Hope it goes better next time," Jackie Duke said.

"What the heck are you woodering your flowers in the dark for?"

"Best time to wooder, when the sun's not on them."

Black walked on the short walkway, then up the six steps to his front door, unlocked the door and went inside. He walked to the fridge, grabbed a National Boh, plopped on a saggy sofa and pouted.

"Damn women. Always teasing."

He drank more cans of National. The last one dropped from his hand as he fell asleep.

14

“It shouldn’t be too difficult to get to him after I get more info. Like the layout of the house,” Baer said over the landline phone to Smithe.

“How are you doing that?”

“A house that looks like his is for sale and I’ll call for an appointment to see it. I’ll ask if the other houses are laid out like that one.”

“Sound’s good. Call if you need us.”

“Of course.”

They hung up.

Baer called the Real Estate Company and secured an appointment.

The next day he was again heading to Essex along I-95N. He met the Real Estate woman, Laurie Franz, at the house for a 10:30 A.M. appointment. He was a little early but she was already there. She walked to his Hyundai SUV as he got out. She extended her hand. “Mr. Rollins, I presume.”

“In the flesh, Miz Franz.” His mole rested on his right cheekbone. No cap covered his curly brown wig. He smiled at her with his brown contacts. He wore a gray plain T-shirt, nothing on it to make him stand out, and blue jeans with a pair of white Nikes. She was dressed in a light gray feminine business suit that complemented her long flowing red hair. Her green eyes were drawn to his. Baer’s eyes were drawn to her white blouse with a semi plunging neckline. Her appearance appealed to the male instincts. *Hmm, not all business. Must be single.*

"So glad you could make it. All the way from Rockville, right?"

"Yes, ma'am."

"Call me Laurie. You said you were planning to move to Essex."

"Yes. Business, you know."

"There is a lot of transfers these days. I think you will like Essex. Would you want to look at the property first?"

"No, I see it. It looks fine, quiet."

"Yes, this is a very nice neighborhood. Well, let's go inside."

"Okay." *Nice neighborhood with a felon living here. I wonder if there are more nice neighbors here like Black.* He knew Essex wasn't a safe city.

As she showed him the inside, he looked at the three bedrooms and the add on in back, the living-room, dining room, etcetera.

"This house is sixteen hundred and thirty square feet and built in nineteen forty-two."

"Nice. Looks sturdy."

They walked around some more and made the usual small talk. Then they went outside. Shaking her hand Baer said, "I will be getting back with you."

"Thank you, Mr. Rollins. Call me anytime."

"And you can call me Tom."

"Okay. Call me anytime—Tom."

"I think you'll be hearing from me—Laurie." *I'd like to, but no way this time.*

He got into his 35% front, 50% rear tinted windows, nondescript Hyundai silver SUV with Maryland plates, that he put on in the morning, and drove off. He never knew if someone, especially a realtor, would copy down his license number. If they did Quark would install a virus on the curious person or police.

On the way back to Shady Oak, his mind was planning on how to get the nice neighbor. By the time he reached his house he knew how he would work it.

The sun shone bright this morning with very few clouds; a beautiful time for Mr. Black to die. It had been two days since he talked with Laurie Franz. He was pleased that she hadn't bothered him with a call on his burner cell phone. Again, he drove the dark tinted 5.0 Mustang—this time with Oklahoma Tags—north on I-95 to Essex. He arrived at the sleazy Super 8 motel on Stemmers Run Road at a little after nine. He nosed the car into the first spot as soon as he came off of Stemmers Run. People would look at the tag and think it belonged there; another out of state visitor. The building in front of the motel was the back of Al's Seafood Restaurant which faced Eastern Boulevard. Baer thought, what a strange set-up that the motel's parking lot was right up to and behind Al's Seafood Restaurant. Al's Seafood parking lot was behind Super 8. Shaking his head he thought again, *strange set-up*. Anyway, it was good cover from the main drag.

Baer put up the sun shades to block the windshield, then he put on his salt and pepper straight hair wig, brown contacts and "traveler" the mole, on the left side of his nose. In his sport coat he had flex-cuffs and latex gloves. He carried a three-and-a-half-inch OTF knife in his dress slack's pocket. He left and locked the car and headed across the street to Enterprise Car Rental on Eastern. He showed the clerk all his fake papers and Oklahoma driver's license. He asked for a silver, gray or white Mitsubishi Mirage and got a gray that could have passed for silver. Good, more confusion for any potential witnesses.

He headed the Mitsubishi south-west on Eastern Boulevard for a two-minute drive to the Art Store's parking lot and parked in the same spot he'd parked the Mustang two days ago. He put a lanyard around his neck with a photo, proclaiming him an Essex city inspector.

When he thought the coast was clear he left the car and walked to the alley behind the store. A few yards later he cut into the brush and moved along the side of Black's saggy rusted four foot high chain link fence. When he was near the back of the house, he grabbed the top of the fence, pole vaulted his legs over and walked to a ladder that laid along the side of the house. The ladder changed his plan a little, no banging on the front door. He put on his rubber gloves picked up the ladder and slammed it against the house and roof by the back door. That brought Kenny Black out the back quickly.

"Hey! What the hell are you doing? Who the hell are you?"

"Bob Roberts, city inspector. I have orders to inspect the outside and inside of your house."

"The hell you do. Get outta here before you need a amblance."

Baer walked towards him holding the lanyard with his picture on it. "With the Covid still running rampant we have to inspect the cleanliness of all houses."

"What fool thought that up? Damn city. Why don't you inspect the crappy businesses on the Avenue?"

"We are, sir." He made a quick scan of the backyards of the neighbor's houses. Clear. He had reached the bottom of the steps and walked up, still holding the false badge. When he got close enough to Black, he pushed him back into the house. Black almost stumbled. The screen door slowly creaked shut.

"Shut up and turn around," Baer commanded.

"What the…"

Baer turned him around and karate chopped both sides of his neck. Black went down hard. They were in the kitchen and Baer grabbed a flimsy chair by the dinette table. He picked Black up and roughly sat him in the chair.

"Hey get off me," Black said coming out of the surprise attack quicker than Baer expected.

Baer went around and bitch slapped him across the face. Black almost fell off the chair but Baer caught him. Black lifted his leg and caught Baer in the groin, knocking the wind out of him, and he doubled over. Black launched a weak left punch into Baer's face. Black was just about to hit him with the right fist when Baer caught Black's knuckles in his left palm and twisted. They both heard the bones break.

"Ow! You son of a bitch!" Black tried to stand and Baer jabbed a right rabbit punch to Black's nose, then a quick left one. That sent Black to the floor. Baer grabbed him and slammed him back into the chair, which fell backward with Black. Pissed, Baer straddled him, bitched slapped him, grabbed a handful of his measly hair and banged his head up and down against the floor. Baer caught himself before he knocked Black unconscious.

Baer got off of Black and struggling, managed to get the chair and Black upright.

"Now shut up, put your hands behind you and listen." Baer was bruised a little but not bleeding. He felt no pain, only anger.

"My wrist, you broke my wrist, you fucker!" Black felt angry, yet fearful.

Baer walked around to Black's back and reached for his flex-cuffs with one hand and held Kenny's unbroken left wrist with the other. Put it over Black's wrist and tightened it. Then went for the broken right one.

"Ahggg, you bastard! Get off my hand! Whatcha gonna do?"

"Shut up or I'll knock you again, you rapist."

Black started to twist and showed some strength. Baer boxed his ears.

"Ow, you..." He started to bring his unbroken hand up to his ear but Baer grabbed it and brought it back again behind Kenny's back and held them both with one hand. With his other hand he zipped a cuff around the right wrist, then tightened that one. Kenny Black didn't struggle. Baer pulled the ties tighter. He pulled out a ten-foot rope and wrapped it around the rapist's arms and chest. Breathing heavy, he tied Black's legs to the chair with another rope. Baer thought, *all this trouble for some info. I better exercise more.*

"Why you doin' this?" Black started to realize he was in *big* trouble. "What are you, a robber? Shit you won't get anything here. Go ahead, rob me. Hurry up, my wrist is killing me."

Baer walked in front of him and looked down at Black's bloody face, blood streaming for his nose and mouth. "Remember a party you went to in Nineteen-sixty-five and you and others, gang banged a classmate."

"I never did no such thing!"

Baer slapped him in the face.

"Ow! Stop, shit-head!"

Another slap.

"Remember a girl named Betty Crenshaw?"

"No." Again a slap. Black shook his head. "I think I remember a Betty but not sure." Black realized he better play nice or he'll get beat again.

"You and others. Clint Zabinski, Scott Turner, Jerry Gannon…"

"Who the fuck are they?"

Baer bitch slapped him again with his palm and back again with the back of his hand.

Mouth bleeding, he hollered, "Okay, okay. I remember now. Yeh, she was a slut."

Another double slap.

"Ow! Stop," he sniffled. "Scott Turner made us take a pledge not to say anything or he was gonna kill us. He checks up on us…for fifty-five years now. I didn't rape her. They wouldn't let me go. Car was crowded. They left me. I went back inside with the girls and thought I could get lucky. No dice. They TOLD me to blow." He spit out some blood and missed Baer by an inch.

Baer was about to hit him again but instead asked, "So you had nothing to do with the rape?"

"No, man. I was mad and left the party. My hand hurts."

"You didn't inform the police?'

"Hell no. I ain't no snitch."

Baer walked behind him. "That makes you guilty as them."

"I toll you, he threatened to kill us if we said anything. What are you, a cop?"

"I'm worse than a cop. So, Turner threatened you with death. Crap, I just killed Clint Zabinski. Maybe I should have told Turner you spilled your guts. Save me the trouble."

"You killed Clint? Shit. Please mister don't kill me. I'll tell the police everything."

"You would do that?" Baer smiled but Black couldn't see.

In pain, Black weakly asked. "So you're not gonna kill me? Are you? My hand hurts."

"Tough, dip shit. I want to give you a message from her husband."

"Husband? She toll her husband? Damn, I see why you're mad."

"Kenny, I'm not mad. I'm just doing a job for him."

"You're a hired gun and he wants you to kill me," he said, whimpering. For the first time Black saw death staring him in the face—and Satan waiting.

"That's my guess, but he wants something worse for you. He wants you strung up by the balls."

"What?" Black, peed in his pants. "Oh, man, please don't do that." Tears ran down his eyes. "Oh, God help me." Now his face really looked like hell, thought Baer.

"I'm not going to do that, Kenny boy. Not my style."

Whimpering, he said, "Good, cause I ain't done nothin'. I've been straight, honest to God."

"Kenny, God and I know you're lying—and you know it. You've done some perverted stuff all your life. Plus, you're an accessory to the raping of a young girl in sixty-five. I see you peed your pants and it stinks."

Black started babbling, pleading, now sobbing, fearing his end was near. Tears, spittle, blood, flying about as he shook his head. "Please mister, tell her I'm sorry," the old man sobbed. "I'm about to shit my pants."

"Don't want that to happen." Baer looked around for a kitchen knife. When he didn't see any he started opening the draws and found them. He grabbed a carving knife out of the drawer, went behind Black and cut the rope but not the flex-cuffs. "I ain't going to shoot you or stab you."

"Thank you, thank you, mister." He made a weird snorting sound.

Still behind Black, Baer put the knife on the counter and said, "This is for your part in raping Betty." With both hands, Baer yanked the rapist off his feet, kicked the chair out of the way and slammed him face first into the dirty bug infested floor. Twisting and dropping down on Black, Baer thrust his knee into the center of Black's upper back and grabbed Black's head with both hands. In one quick burst of strength Baer brought all of his weight down below the back of Black's head and yanked up on his chin. The noise of the neck as it snapped sounded like a brittle tree branch broke over one's knee. Breathing heavy, Baer rose and stood over Black. "You piece of shit." Baer heard an eerie gurgling sound that escaped from Black's throat. The dying man's eyes opened wider and wider until it looked like they would pop out. Twenty-five seconds later the gurgling stopped. Black's body lay lifeless on the dirty, dead bug infested, now also bloody floor.

Baer looked around for paper and found an envelope. After a quick search he spotted a pen and wrote left-handed on the envelope, *child rapist.* He shoved the pen through the envelope and found a soft spot between Black's spine and right shoulder. *This bastard could have put the others away.* Then with extreme force, stabbed the pen and envelope into Black.

He gathered the rope and ties and made sure he didn't leave anything. He stuck them in his coat pockets. He cleaned and sanitized his mess to make sure he wasn't leaving any DNA. He took off his gloves and shoved them in his coat pocket. He grabbed a small rag, then Baer peeked out the back door. Seemed all clear. He opened it with the rag, locked it, and stuffed the rag into his pocket. He briskly walked to the fence. Suddenly, the man next door leaned out from his door, and yelled, "Everythink okay?"

Baer turned and held up his photo. "Everything's fine. City Inspector."

The man waved and went back into the house.

Baer got in the rental, took the rag out of his pants pockets, threw it on the seat. He headed back to Enterprise to return the SUV. After arriving, he grabbed the rag and wiped the steering wheel, wiped the keys and wrapped them in Kleenex, then stuffed the rag back into his pocket. Went inside, gave the keys back, by opening the Kleenex and dropped them on the counter, got his receipt, then walked to the corner of Eastern Boulevard and Stemmers Run. Crossing Stemmers Run against the light, he quickly stepped into his Mustang at the Super 8. He pushed the start button and left, heading for home. He pulled into a rest area on I-95 between Baltimore and Washington. He had already taken the wig off, now he removed the mole and stored it in its special box. Next, he took out the brown contacts and boxed them. He shed his sport coat, threw it in the back seat and walked towards the men's room.

When he got home, he called Smith on the scramble phone—the newest type. This new type was much easier, no recording messages, then calling, and all the other crap that went with the old-style scrambler. Just straight through.

"Well, John, Kenny Black no longer lives in this world."

"Any problems."

"He put up a good struggle. Otherwise, smooth as silk, like Clint Zabinski. Who knows when someone will find Black. He didn't have many friends that we know of. But Scott Turner held the threat of death over him, actually all of them. He keeps in touch with them once a year."

"Interesting. Well one day someone will find his stinking body or bones. Who's next?"

"Can you hold on while I fix a drink?" Baer asked.

"Yeah, go ahead, but make it snappy."

Baer came back in two minutes. "You there?"

"Yeah. Who's next?"

"After fighting with Black, I think I need a vacation so I'm going to Florida in two days."

Smithe said, "Hmm. Flying or driving?"

"Flying this time, just to reconnoiter. Maybe drive to do the job. I'm playing all of this by ear, you know. Turner's dossier says he's a born-again Christian. I'll see if he is."

"What if he is? How you going to find out?" Smithe sounded apprehensive.

"I'll talk to his pastor and I'll try to follow him around. With this new info, I think it's just a cover. It looks like he might be a ring leader of some sort by keeping tabs with this group of rapists."

"I'll relay the progress report to Witkowski and have him advance it to the client."

"Sounds good, John. No names. I'm going to hit the sack. Good night."

"I know no names. You had a fight with him, you said?"

"Nothing I couldn't handle."

"Well, a fight costs more if the job wasn't a slam, bam, thank you ma'am. Got any injuries?"

"Very minor. It was a little rough but that comes with the territory."

"Just the same, I'm upping the cost."

"You're the accountant."

"Okay. Just be careful."

"Always. Night."

Baer finished his drink. "I got to exercise more."

15

"That's enough, Jesse, leave her alone or I'll throw you out," Sam, the bartender hollered.

"Let me go, Jesse, you creep," Doris said. She finally got loose and yelled, "Sam, throw the bum out. I'm tired of his shit."

Sam came from around the bar and headed in Jesse's direction. Jesse pushed himself up from the table, wobbling and laughing. "I'm going Sam. Doan need no help," he slurred. "I love you, Doris." He zigged zagged towards the bar.

Sam grabbed him by the arm and said, "Let's go, Jesse. Come back next week." Sam reached the door, opened it and put Jesse out and pointed him in the direction to his house. He wasn't rough with the old geezer, just irritated. "Go sleep it off." He gently pushed Jesse onward.

Jesse stumbled along waving a hand. "Sleep." Tonight he was unusually calm.

Sam watched him a minute to make sure he was still moving in the right direction. Then he went back in.

Doris walked up to Sam. "Sam, if you don't keep him out, I'll quit."

"Doris, I pay you good and you get good tips. Just holler like you did and I'll send him on his way. I won't let him do anything to you. You're good for my business. He's just a poor old stumble bum…with money."

"Humph! I don't know where he gets it."

"Neither do I and I don't care. I take care of you. Let him be."

Baer woke to the sound of his fax machine working. He sat up and stretched. He looked at the clock, 8:03 A.M. It was either Smithe or the geeks sending him something. He strolled to his office. Looking at the machine he saw, the geeks. They sent another Dossier. When the machine stopped, he reached for the paper. *Hmm. Jesse Delaney.* He read it.

Dossier:	Jesse M. Delaney. Intel date, Oct., 2020
Born:	January 8, 1945
Place:	Arlington, VA. Arlington General Hospital.
Childhood Home:	Arlington until Feb. 28, 1956; Dundalk, MD. since Feb. 29, 1956
Graduated:	No. Dropped out at 14
Nickname:	none, Jesse only; idol, Jesse James
Employments:	Multiple odd jobs, including but not limited to, construction, encyclopedia salesman, liquor delivery driver.
Married:	Gladys Koosler, 1967, Divorced.
	Gloria Snodgrass, 1975, Divorced.
	Carla Cooper, 1979, Divorced.
	None other known. Several live ins through the years.
Domicile:	405 Brad Street, Parkville, MD. 21234 Grandparents former house.
Land Line:	410-555-3870

Cell:	None
Criminal Record(s):	Arrested selling alcohol to minors, 1965, 1968, 1972, 1980. Attempted rape of young girls, twice, 1981, 1986. Sexual assaults. Aggravated assault on police officers, 1975, 1988, 1998, 2005, 2016. Arrested and charged, each crime. Jail time & fines. Considered dangerous nuisance.
Service Record(s):	none
END	

"The geeks finally found him," muttered Jake. He called Smithe.

"So the geeks found ol' Jesse Jerk," Baer stated.

"Yeah. Really it was Quark, but no matter. What are you thinking?"

"I think I'll leave him for last. Hell, he's seventy-five now and they say he's *dangerous?*"

"I think he's in pretty good shape for his age. He still assaults the cops but they just punch him out and leave him on his front porch. They don't bother taking him to jail now. Too much paperwork."

"Does he still hit the sauce?" Baer asked.

"What I understand is yes and often."

"Damn, I might have to change my vacation. I don't want him to die before I get to him. They call him dangerous? That's a laugh and a half."

"Understood. Do what you want with him."

Chuckling he said, "Maybe I'll send him to Oklahoma, if he's tougher than Kenny Black."

Smithe growled, "Don't do anything fancy and get caught."

"Never happen." Jake Baer laughed.

"Never say never, my boy."

Jesse lived in a run-down row house in a sleezy part of Parkville, MD. Off from Harford Road there was a little pub that Jesse frequented. Baer thought it was closer to Baltimore than Parkville. What the heck, boundaries meant nothing to him. Delaney was known to "live" at the bar, so he would scope it out just in case Delaney was there—and have a drink. Baer entered the bar and picked a small table close to the door, facing it, a wall behind him. He scanned around the dimly lit place and didn't see Delaney. He had studied the picture of the creep and he looked like a creep. All of the dossiers came with their latest photos. Some were mug shots.

It had been another hot, hazy, muggy, pre-fall day in Baltimore, just the type of weather Baer hated. He thought it made him meaner. He had noticed that other people seemed more agitated with this type of weather. Made it more uncomfortable when wearing a disguise. Jake Baer sucked it up. He had business to take care of. *Neither rain, nor sleet, nor ice, or hot humid weather keeps me from my appointed rounds.* He chuckled to himself.

Baer was not himself again tonight—in disguise; dark hair, mole and black contacts. He was trying new contacts that were specially made for him. These were very dark. When looking into Jake's eyes the bartender saw black. Jake saw everything in normal lighting, nothing was dark. They were advanced night vision goggles in contact size. The ex-senator had all kinds of clandestine options, scientists, inventors, working for him.

If Delaney didn't walk in tonight, maybe a sweet thing would and he'd get lucky. He finished his Heineken.

The bartender brought another beer over when Jake signaled. The man started to talk with him. "Not from around here, are you?" It was a light night so he had time to chat.

There was no way Baer could blow him off. That would definitely raise a red flag. Got to be friendly. So he said, "No. I'll be visiting a friend tomorrow in Towson."

"I asked because I knew you weren't a regular. I like talking to people from different places when they stop in here. Hope you don't mind."

"Don't mind a-tall. I'll buy you a beer."

"The owner won't let us drink on the job. Thanks anyway." Then he asked, "If you don't mind my asking, where're you from?"

Baer minded but he played the game. "Boston."

"I thought I detected a little accent. Nothing wrong with an accent, ain't it."

They did some more small talk and Baer wished he would go away.

Ten minutes later, while they were talking and Baer nursing his beer, Jesse walked in. He looked like his mug shot. He followed him with his eyes. Jesse sat at the bar, turned towards the barkeep and loudly said "Hey Sam. Doris here?"

The barkeep replied, somewhat annoyed, "No. Her night off."

Jesse banged his fist on the bar. "Damn, slut. Said she'd be here."

"Watch your mouth Jesse and I'll get you your regular." Sam got up, said "'scuse me" to Baer.

"I don't want Helen."

"Your beer, Michelob."

"Oh. Yeah. Bring her up," he laughed. "Then after that, start bringing Natty Boh."

Baer sat grinning. *What a lush. Should be easy to get him.*

Delaney had turned around and leaned against the bar scanning the joint. He looked hard at Baer.

"Who you grinning at, fool?"

"No one." He paused. "Jesse."

"You grinning at me? Ain't chew?'

"Like I said…no one."

"Say, you got some sass, mister."

"Jesse, here's your beer," said Sam.

Sneering Jesse said, "Put it on the stranger's tab."

"Now Jesse don't go bothering the customers again or you're outta here."

Jesse grabbed the beer bottle and took a long pull. "Put my whole tab I'll run up tonight on the stranger's tab. And forget the Boh. I'll stick with the Mick, since the stranger'll pay for it."

The bartender was just about to say something when Baer said, "My pleasure. Keep 'em coming."

Sam shrugged and walked away.

Jesse walked to Baer's table, pulled out a chair and sat. "You know, you're not bad for a fool, fool."

In this business you have to play it cool. Jesse wanted to start trouble. Well he found it and Baer thought this would be easier than he expected. He stared hard at Jesse's miserable ten-day old beard, and watery eyes. Jesse's goading didn't bother him. Came with the job. Besides he was just another worthless piece of trash to get rid of.

"Whatcha looking at? Take a pix chur, it'll last longer." Jesse started laughing.

"Bring him another, Sam" Baer hollered.

"Shit, man. You're okay. Where you from?"

"Jersey City." Baer smiled. Baer gave out city names like candy.

The new bottle of beer arrived. Jesse took a pull. "Reminds me. What did Della wear?"

"I haven't a clue." Baer eyed him. This guy is wacko.

"She wore a new jersey." He laughed so hard he started hacking.

After he caught his breath he asked, "Now what did she drink?"

"Don't know."

"A mini soda." Jesse laughed and hacked. "Get it? Made that part up muh-self." He laughed again and coughed. He took a swig.

Baer thought, *don't die on me, fool.*

"Where you staying?" Jesse asked after his bout of hacking.

"Oh, down the street." Bear hoped Jesse would get looped quick.

"Hey, you can stay with me."

Grinning, Baer said, "Can't, have an early meeting tomorrow morning. Thanks anyway." Baer rose.

"Hey where you goin'? We just got started."

"Got to get up early." He walked over to the bar and gave Sam a twenty. "I'll be back tomorrow if it cost more, but I think that should do it."

"It's more than enough, cause I'm gonna cut him off soon."

"Then keep the change." Baer headed for the door.

"Hope to see you again," hollered Delaney.

Baer waved without looking back. Outside he looked around for cameras. He didn't see any. No other businesses, and the houses didn't have any. Probably too poor or they didn't care. He walked to his SUV, stepped in and waited. He had parked on the street so he could keep a close eye on the bar's door in his rear-view mirror. He planned to confront Delaney. Hopefully he'd walk his way. Reaching for the glove compartment he grabbed his K-Bar in its scabbard. He placed it in his door panel pouch. He kept glancing in the rear-view mirror. Surveillance waiting wasn't his favorite work, but it paid good. He took the contacts out and placed them in its special box.

Fifty-four minutes later Delaney came staggering out and Baer was elated that he was heading his way, coming from behind. Baer slid down the passenger window. Delaney reach alongside and Baer hollered, "Hey, Jesse."

Delaney stopped and squinted. "Who that?"

"It's me, Jesse, I bought your drinks." Baer wiped the sweat from his eyes.

Jesse walked up to the window. "Yeah?"

"I'll take you up on the offer to stay the night, if the invites still open."

"Sure. Iffin, you buy us a pint first."

"You bet. Stay and watch the car while I get it."

"Sure." He leaned against the SUV to help prop himself.

In a short time, Baer came back with the pint. "Hop in. Where do you live?"

In the SUV Jesse said, "Up the street in a row." Meaning a row house in Baltimore. Townhouse everywhere else.

Baer drove a short way to Brad Street and pulled in front of it when he was told. His house looked the worst. The number five was missing making it 40. The rapist's house looked like it needed a major renovation. His neighbors probably wished he'd move. They're going to get their wish.

Before they got out Delaney said, "Now look, I ain't no queer, so no shit."

"I'm not either, so don't worry. I like talking about women. Let's go."

Baer gave Jesse the pint, he took the K-Bar and stuck it in his back pocket. No porch lights were on. Good.

They walked into a pig sty that smelled of mold and something else Baer couldn't identify. Maybe a dead rodent.

"You can sleep on that couch."

"Great. Thanks." Baer thought it was a piss poor looking couch. Good thing he wasn't going to sleep there.

"I'll get some glasses. You'll have to rinse yours. By the way I didn't get your name."

"Smart. Winston Smart." He gave one of his favorite aliases, even though Delaney would never be able to tell anyone.

They sat, with Baer pulling out a dinette chair with his foot. Delaney sat on a filthy, vomit-stained chair and started drinking. Delaney drank more than Baer. Baer took one small sip.

"So Jesse, let's talk about women…and girls. Did you ever do any girls?"

"Sure. When I was younger. Oh, boy, I'll never forget the one I had when I was twenty, I think. Yes, I was twenty. I had a beautiful car. A red Chevy Super Sport. Oh man the girls went for that."

"I bet."

"Lost that. Shit, I lost everything. Iffin' I had more luck. Never had no luck with wimmin or jobs." He took a drink. "When I was younger, man, I had a time. I member some high school girl had a party and I got the booze for 'em." He finished his glass and poured more. "Some high school guys were there, 'bout sixteen, seventeen, and they was getting high quick. Somebody said for us to take a ride in my car and they brought along this sweet young piece with them. Named Betty. I'll never forget her or that night."

Delaney talked on, and went into detail. The more he drank and talked, the angrier Baer became. He listened only because he didn't know the whole story. Now he was really pissed, and he didn't know Betty personally. This made it real. These ass holes deserved to die. He never had any regrets about his line of work. He still had no regrets after hearing Delaney's version. He had enough.

"Stop." Baer stood and pulled out latex gloves from his pocket.

"Wha...?" Delaney looked dumbfounded as he watched Baer put them on his hands. Bleary eyed, he saw Baer retrieve a knife from his back pocket. Baer slid it out of the scabbard and put the scabbard back into his pocket.

"Whatcha gonna do with that Bowie knife?" Even sitting, Jesse was weaving a little.

"This here is Mister Justice, for Betty, the sixteen-year-old girl you raped with your predator friends. Time to die." He stared at the rapist.

"Huh? Wait. I never meant her no harm. We was just horny kids."

"Guess what, Jesse, you did her and her husband, more harm than you could imagine."

Even drunk, Delaney looked up and pleaded, "Please don't kill me. Tell her I'm sorry." He started to cry. Drunk or not, he bawled like a baby. "Scott made me do it," he lied.

Baer thought, they're always sorry but never once did any offer some kind of restitution, way back then, when they all had a chance. The bastards were only sorry because someone found out and was going to kill them. So far everyone of them blubbered when they faced death.

Baer reached for Delaney's shirt and jerked him up. He spun him around and kicked his legs out from under him. Baer followed him down and smashed his right knee into Delaney's back. Delaney couldn't put up even a drunken fight as Baer lifted his forehead with his left hand exposing his neck to the blade of justice. "For Betty." With one quick stroke Baer deeply slit his throat from ear to ear, literally. Blood poured out and Delaney tried to reach for his throat but Baer didn't let him. He laid the knife down and held Delaney's forehead back with both hands. Bent that way Delaney's flailing arms were useless. Delaney was choking, gasping, making a variety of weird sounds. Baer held his head back until he soon, died.

Baer used different methods of killing the rapists making it harder to connect the killings, if the police would even have a chance of connecting them.

Bear washed his gloves and knife. Then he found a rag and wrapped his gloves in it and stuck them into his pocket. He put the K-Bar back in its sheath and pocket. He grabbed the glass he drank from and smashed it on the floor and ground it with his heel. *See if you can find prints on that.* Baer went to the front door, pulled out his shirt and grabbed the handle, locking it. He checked before he went out. Clear. Pulled the door shut and casually walked to his SUV.

An hour and a half later he was back in his peaceful home. He called Smithe on the scrambler. Smithe answered on the second ring. "Jake."

"Don't you ever sleep?"

"Sure, with one eye and ear open. Give me the skinny."

"Jesse Delaney is no longer with us."

"So that leaves Jerry Gannon and Scott Turner?"

"Right. Gannon's in Takoma Park, Maryland, and Turner's in Rotonda West, Florida." Baer thought for a second. "You know, John, this assignment has been pretty easy so far. Well, except for Black."

"Jake, you just broke the spell. Good work and goodnight. We'll talk tomorrow."

After they hung up, Baer went right to bed and slept like a rock.

16

The next day Baer started working out strategies for Gannon and Turner. He decided it was time to visit Florida. He booked a flight to Southwest Florida International Airport. What he considered a phony health pandemic wasn't as pandemic in Florida. Everything was wide open. Around the country all kinds of flus and colds were way way down. But suicides and murders were way way up. Life and death have ways of balancing out, he thought.

Smithe had called earlier to let him know that the bodies of Black and Delaney haven't been reported. So not found yet. Probably would take a while. Baer would never be on the radar for the three killings, he meant, punishments.

Two days after Black was killed his neighbor thought it was strange that he hadn't seen Kenny lately. Kenny would at least water his few measly looking plants every day and maybe sit out back with a six pack. Not bothering anyone but a weird person, to him. The neighbor, Jackie Duke, would say hi and he'd wave. That was it. Good neighbor to have really. No bother, no trouble, no women visiting or anyone visiting, except for the city inspector. He wondered what that was about. He didn't get a visit from the city. Thank God.

Curiosity overtook him so Jackie decided to take a chance and see if Kenny was home. He walked to Black's front door and knocked. No answer. Maybe the doorbell works. He tried it. It worked. No one came. He rang again. No one. It's nine o'clock, and his car was there, Kenny should still be home.

Jackie took another chance and walked around back and knocked on the door. Nothing. He tried the door knob. Locked. He peered through the sheer curtains on the door's two small windows. He saw something on the floor, kind of in the dining area. With this house, from the back door you could see all the way through and see a little of the front room. The clump he saw was between the back door and the front room. He squinted to get a better look. He smelled a slight strange order that he didn't recognize. Jackie squinted again—this time it looked like he saw feet, shoes on. Shit!

Jackie grabbed the knob again but it wouldn't turn. He knew something was wrong and broke the glass with his elbow. The putrid smell hit him immediately and he almost vomited. Composed, he put his hand over his nose—not much help. He reached in and unlocked the door. He pushed it open and covered his face within the crook of his arm. He slowly approached, saw that it was Kenny. He gaged and ran out the back.

Back at this house he dialed 911.

Two white Baltimore County Ford Police Interceptor SUVs from the Essex precinct arrived in four minutes. One of the County officers, Peter Nelson, climbed out of his car and two officers exited the other car, a man and woman. Jackie Duke waited for them in front of Black's house on the sidewalk. He wiped the sweat from his forehead as the officers approached.

"This is the house officers." He jerked his thumb at the house. "I'll take you 'round back cause that's where I got in." He started walking.

"Hold up there, sir," commanded officer Nelson, who had one stripe on his sleeve. "First, stay here and tell us what you saw and did."

Duke spoke quickly, like time was running out. The officer had to slow him down.

After Duke finished the officer said, "Okay, now show us."

They walked around to the back. At the bottom of the steps the woman officer said, "Stay here."

Nelson stepped up to the door, looked at the damage and said, "You broke this, Mister…?"

"Duke, Jackie Duke. Yes, sir, the only way I could get in and see. Also, he liked to be called Duke. Everyone knew him as Duke. So, if you ask around make sure they know it's Kenny and not me."

The woman officer had her notepad in her hand and wrote everything down.

"Did you touch anything?" she asked.

"Only the outside of the doorknob. Oh, and the inside to unlock it."

"We'll get your prints later to keep you separated from any other latent's," Nelson said.

Duke looked at him quizzically.

"Means we'll check your fingerprints with any others that we find. We know we'll find his. Taking yours, we can rule you out as a suspect. Any other prints we find could be the killers."

"Ah," approved Duke, nodding his head.

"Don't watch any TV?" the female officer asked rhetorically.

"No, not much. My hobby is stamp collecting, so that's what I do mostly."

Nelson and the female officer, Julie, walked slowly into the house. Before they reached the body, they were breathing through their mouths. Didn't help much. Nelson asked, "Who the hell collects stamps anymore?" He gagged a little.

"We know he does. Good thing. Keeps an eye on the neighborhood."

"*Right*. Didn't keep this stiff from getting killed."

They had finally crooked their arms over their noses approaching carefully and stood at the body, observing the gruesome victim.

"What the hell," Officer Nelson bent closer to the body. "Stabbed in the back with a pen and paper. Says, child rapist. Damn."

"Look at his eyes, Pete," said the woman officer.

"Damned if I know what made his eyes do that," Officer Nelson said. "I'm calling in the Medical Examiner and a detective. Let's get outta here."

When they stepped outside, they both took deep breaths and tried to clear their sinuses. Nelson finally asked Julie if she had all the pertinent info.

"Yes, got it all. His story, that is."

Duke said, "Man, I can smell him out here. I wish the wind would blow."

"Thank you for your help and concern, Mister Duke. We'll get back with you if we need more."

"That poor man. Never had any problems with him." Duke stood and didn't make a move.

Officer Nelson put his arm around his shoulder and walked him to the front sidewalk. "Let us know if you think of anything else."

"Okay." Duke slowly walked back to his house glancing back at Black's house. Shaking his head, he mumbled, "Poor man." Then a sickening thought struck him. *It coulda been me.*

The Medical Examiner and the detective arrived at the same time. Nelson told the M.E. to go in the back way. Then he turned to the detective and said, "Julia'll read you her notes as to what happened. I haven't a clue. The vic looks weird."

Turning to the other officers, detective Jablonski said, "Okay, you two search the grounds, then canvass the neighbors."

"Got it."

Officer Julie Barton said, "Start at the back steps and go towards the fence. The wit said the man jumped the fence when he left the house."

"You mean Duke saw the killer?"

"Don't know if he's the killer. Duke said he checked on Black two days after he saw the city inspector."

"The city inspector?" Nelson questioned."

"Check the grounds officer," said detective Jablonski. Then he turned to Julie.

"What's this about a city inspector?"

"That's what Duke said. The guy said he was a city inspector and Duke told me he hoped he wasn't next…to be inspected. He wasn't thinking about being killed. Duke is assuming that the inspector didn't do this."

"Yeah, well, Duke's not a detective. In a minute I'll go take a look for myself. Don't want to bother the M.E. right now. Did he get a description?"

"Yes, he had short brown hair and a blue sport coat. And sunglasses. He was white and a good looking fellow."

"A good looking fellow. Hmm. Counting me there's a lot of those running around." He winked at her.

"Yeh, yeh. I had to ask him because he couldn't really give a good description."

Detective Jablonski kept it up. "Do you know how many good-looking white guys with short brown hair there are?"

"Yeh, I see a lot of 'em all the time," she said sarcastically.

"Exactly." He smiled at her. "Did he see where he went after the guy jumped the fence?"

"No, but he assumed to the art gallery parking lot."

"Why would a city inspector park there when he can park in front of the vic's house? *If* he was a city inspector."

"I don't know, you're the detective."

"I was thinking out loud, officer." He smiled. *She's cute.* "Tell Nelson and the others to check the alley and that parking lot. See if there are any cameras, owner might know something, etcetera. I'm going inside and take a look. And if you would, please help them out." He winked.

"I'll get right on it."

He watched her go for a few seconds then went into the house.

"Whatcha got?" He looked at the body and said, "Whoa. What happened to his eyes?"

"Far as I can tell, he got his neck broke," the M.E. said.

Detective Jablonski said, "Is that a pen in his back with a note?"

"You're good, detective. Yes."

"Ah, shut-up. What's it say? I'm not bending over."

"Child rapist. I'll be able to tell more when I get him on the slab, but the way his neck was broke, it's a professional job. Like a Navy Seal, or Army Rangers professional."

"What? I got to check and see if he'd been in the service. Might have pissed off some high brass or low stripes."

An officer stuck his head in the door, "Amblance is here, Doc."

"Okay, tell them to bring the gurney and take him to the morgue."

"Right."

"I think I'll stay and check his place out and see if I can figure out why he was killed by professional military."

"Knock yourself out." The M.E. left.

Detective Jablonski walked around the house trying to get a sense of the dead man. Nothing. Seemed like a loser. He watched the crime scene people take photos and dust for prints. *If the guy who killed him was a professional, I'll get nothing.* After looking around for a few minutes more, he left for the precinct.

At the precinct, Jablonski searched the computer for Blacks' service records. Nothing came up. Using his iPhone, he then called the Baltimore County government offices to check on home inspections. Nothing on any kind of inspection. Disappointed, he thanked the bureaucrat and disconnected.

He talked to himself softly. "I've got nothing."

17

S itting in one of Smithe's comfortable chairs in the den with a mixed drink in his hand, Jake Baer was surprised at what the former Oklahoma senator just said.

"You mean you are actually thinking of moving back to Oklahoma, with the underground, and the geeks?"

"Yeah. Virginia is not like it used to be. I'm afraid they will follow in Maryland's footsteps and go Liberal." He sighed. "Too many trees here anyway, can't see a damn thing. Besides, I want to be buried in Oklahoma."

"Trees are good for my line of work, but let me know for sure, cause I'll go back too."

"Well, it's not going to be like tomorrow."

Laughing he said, "Whew. I still have some jobs to do."

Smithe spit out his gum into an ashtray. "Who's next on your list?"

"The airlines are back in business so I've got a flight booked tomorrow for Florida. Check out Scott Turner."

"The born-again Christian?"

"That's the one."

"That's all I want to know."

Taking a swig of his drink Baer said, "That's all I'm going to tell you."

"You are covering your trail good, right?"

"Does a bear shit in the woods?"

Laughing Smithe said, "I don't know, do you?"

Baer just smiled at his double entendre.

"You know I'm leaving you all my worldly possessions when I go." Smithe elaborated.

Baer couldn't say a word.

"I think Oklahoma would be the best and safest place for our, then yours, continuing operations."

"I think you'll be around for a while."

"Maybe, but in the meantime, I'm looking for a great spot. Probably eastern part of the state. More trees."

"I think I have to agree with you. I thought you wanted less trees."

"I can still see the country side. You know the trees are shorter and not too dense. Well, some places they're dense."

"Also, closer to our Predator drone in the western part of the state."

They talked some more about future plans.

Baer said, "I'm going home and hit the sack. Got an early flight tomorrow."

"Right. Be careful."

"Always."

Baer woke up in a good mood. He even whistled while he did his bathroom chores. The airlines made it easy for him to travel incognito, everyone had to wear a mask and he would add glasses and brown contacts, also— traveler, the mole.

Placing the straight hair, black wig on, he smiled. He placed his brown contacts in, then he put "traveler" on the right side of his cheek below the eye, on the bone. Even wearing a mask, he decided to go disguised, too many cameras and TSA. Less chance for a slip up. TSA might ask people to remove masks so they could match up driver's license photos. He added a limp for his right leg by placing a small smooth stone inside his shoe—using a cane with an eagle head handle. The cane was lined inside with lead to hide a short sword. His disguises were made by professional make-up artists that the geeks had connections with.

Besides the limp he would add a slight stoop which would make him look shorter.

He packed a change of clothes into a small hard suitcase in case he had to stay longer than he planned. This was going to be a quick overnighter. He left Shady Oak for Dulles International Airport at five o'clock. He drove southwest on VA. state highway 674 then onto VA. 267, the Dulles Access Road. Driving fast it took him 20 minutes to get there. He parked his SUV in the short-term parking.

As Baer boarded the plane from the jetway the hostess greeted everyone at the door. At the same time, the other hostess, in the middle of the plane, was also eyeing the passengers. They were looking for ABPs, able-bodied passengers that could help them in an emergency. They were also looking for anyone who might cause trouble. This flight had no armed undercover security. Jane Stafford, at the door, ran her eyes over Baer as he limped by. Quickly and professionally, she had sized him up as a non-threat or a possible future disturbance since he was limping and used a cane.

Not looking at her, Baer smiled but his face was covered with a mask. He found his seat.

The Southwest Boeing 737-700 airliner took off on schedule: 6:10 A.M. It looked like rain for Chantilly. Baer hoped the pilot would climb above the storm. He settled himself in seat 21C, an aisle seat with plenty of legroom. He was on the left side of the aisle facing front. Everyone had a mask on and he hated wearing his but it was good cover. His seat was three rows from the rear lavatories, which made him happy. One of the three women attendants walked by heading towards the front. Her red jacket covered some of her derrière but the rest looked great. Her black straight skirt came just above the knees, and she wore black heels. The shoulder length blonde hair touched her shoulders, swaying provocatively.

He eyed her again on her way back to the galley and noticed the front of her skirt had tasteful red and blue stripes on her right side, from the waist to the bottom of her skirt. The airline colors. The front of her jacket was zipped from neck to just below the waist. Her eyes were bright blue and smiling at him. Shame he couldn't see her nose and mouth—yet. He would, he thought.

She walked by again and Baer said, "Ma'am."

She stopped. "Yes, sir?"

"Do you serve something to wet my whistle?" He pulled down his mask and smiled.

"Sure, I'll get you a cup of water."

"No, I mean, like a real drink." He winked.

"We don't serve those anymore on flights because..."

He raised his hand to stop her. He motioned for her to come closer to his mouth. She bent a little and he whispered, "I know you have something to put in my water. Right?"

She raised up and padded him on the shoulder. She must have liked his looks, mole and all, because she went back to the galley. She came back with a medium size cup filled with ice and a brown liquid.

"Here's your water, sir." After he took the cup, she pulled down her mask, exposing full lips colored light red and a straight medium nose. She bent down to his ear and said, "I don't do this for anyone. I could get in trouble." *Handsome face and muscular. Too bad he had a limp.*

The tough guy melted quicker than ice cubes in the sun. He almost stammered but smiling he managed to say in a normal voice, "Thanks, hon."

She stood, put her mask back up, and sashayed up the aisle with Baer's eyes following her. He drank it in one gulp. Almost choked but caught it. *Man, this is good stuff. And her too.*

He felt his heart race like it never did before. He didn't know it then but he just fell in love.

When she walked back, she asked, "Do you want more water?"

He said, "Sure, please." *What the hell am I doing?*

She gave him the drink with a note. He took both together and no one was the wiser. She walked back to the galley. He opened the note. *I have a layover tonight. Want to have a drink?* He thought, Oh, shit.

The next time Jane Stafford walked by him on her way to the galley, she squeezed his shoulder. Baer had been thinking and now was the time to put his plan into action, since she was alone. He left his seat with his cane and limped back to the Galley.

"Hi Mr. George," Jane said sweetly.

"Hi. And what is your name, since I'm at a disadvantage here."

"Jane Stafford." She stuck out her hand.

Baer took it and kissed the top of her hand. "I'm charmed."

"Oh, my," she giggled. "I see you have a limp. What happened?"

"Just a war wound you might say."

"How sad. What war?"

"Actually, I got it on the job chasing someone in Madrid. I'm with Interpol."

That was his cover but he didn't expect to use it for a chance meeting with a beautiful woman, 34,000 feet in the air. He pulled out his fake badge and showed her. The address said Lyon, France.

"Oh my. You must be a tough guy." She smiled. *And an ABP.*

"Not tough enough for missing a bullet." He didn't like lying to her but it was part of who he was, and it was part of the job.

"Well, can you meet me after I get off work," she said. "I have some time."

There was that smile again. "I'd love to but I can't…this time. I'm on a tight schedule and will be leaving Sunday at three fifteen."

"Back to Dulles?" she asked.

"Yes."

"Good. I'll see you on that flight. My home base is Dee Cee."

"Great, mine is close to Alexandria."

"Oh? Not Lyon?"

"No. That's the home office."

The pilot announced over the intercom, "We will be landing in fifteen minutes. The weather is muggy with possible showers. Put all trays up and seats in the upright position. The attendants will assist anyone that needs help. Thank you for flying Southwest Airlines. We enjoyed having you."

Baer took her hand in both of his. "Auf wiedershen, and, 'till we meet again."

She followed him back to his seat.

"Make sure you fasten your seat belt," she said smiling.

"I will. I don't want to fall out of the plane."

She slapped him on the arm and walked up the aisle making sure everyone was buckled in.

They landed at Southwest Florida International Airport and disembarked. He grabbed Jane's hand, "See you later." and quickly let go as he went by and into the jetway. She smiled.

When they landed, clouds were forming and threatening some showers as usual. He quickly went to a car rental area before the showers hit. He limped, using his cane, to the Thrifty Car Rental and picked out a car.

It did feel warm and slightly muggy as he got into his rental. The sun shone bright. Large puffy white clouds dotted the sky, some darker ones forming on the horizon. They usually brought a shower or two as they moved north-east. Baer thought he could smell the sea. Refreshing. As was the stewardess. Yes, he used the old terminology. He considered himself a sexist, which meant he was protective toward all women. *There were no women Navy Seals. One tried in 2017 but soon dropped out. No shit, Sherlock.*

He drove the Terminal Access Road to I-75. He continued on I-75, drove over the Peace River and shortly took exit 170 to FL. 776.

Later on, he drove over the Myakka River. In short order he arrived at Rotonda West, taking him 1 hour and 15 minutes to make the 67-mile trip. He hadn't eaten in a while and took out a *Kind Dark Chocolate Breakfast* bar, he brought, to give him some energy. He munched on that while looking for the address.

It didn't take him long to find 4425 Rotary Circle. The main street was shaped like an old wagon wheel, the side streets being the thick spokes, Turner lived on the rim itself. Modern stucco Spanish style houses were the majority and his was no exception. *Damn he did good for himself. With no criminal record Scott thinks he's scot free.* Baer smiled at his wit.

Baer drove by the house slowly. He knew behind Turner's house was a creek the residents used for small boating fun. Baer's conundrum was getting in the house or getting Turner out. There was no way to snipe him. People watch the water more than the streets. It might have to be a front door attack but he'd have to think that out. It was a double type glass door with a left side entrance. He really didn't like the idea already.

The front yard had a couple of palm trees and a white Chevy 4X4 was parked outside of the double garage. Does he have more vehicles in the garage? Is he even home or on vacation? The geeks will have to find out.

Baer noticed a number of cameras outside a few houses, and a number of houses also had Ring. He'd have to lure him away from his house. Right now he couldn't see any other way.

He brought a portable dash cam with him and turned it on. He backed into a driveway across from the house, paused, then pulled out and headed in the direction he came from. Next stop, Turner's church. All caught on the dash cam. Today was Friday, he'd get a motel close and go to the services Sunday.

He headed for the Sun Coast Inn motel. It was close and inexpensive. He didn't care that it was inexpensive—it was close.

In the parking lot of the Motel he found a secluded spot to take off his disguise. He put the disguise in a bag, carried it and his suitcase into the motel. In his room he freshened up, went to a restaurant and ate quickly. He wanted to get back to the motel and planned the details of going to Turner's church Saturday morning to check out the surroundings.

He now figured out he would have had enough time to be with Jane Stafford, Saturday, but that would distract him. He needed to stay focused. He wasn't getting paid to dally with women. Damn.

Sunday morning, he packed his suitcase and put it in the car. He had enough time for that and catch the 3:15 P.M. flight back to Dulles. He checked out of the motel at seven and looked for breakfast and found a Burger King. He still had plenty of time. Services didn't start at the Rotonda Lutheran Church of Fellowship until 9:30.

He walked in at 9:10 and the church was half full. He sat in the last row. As he waited only a few more entered before the services started. He knew he would probably be noticed as a newcomer. At 9:30 the Reverend whomever—he didn't remember the name and didn't care—opened with, "Good morning. Let's start with *Rock of Ages.*" Everyone stood. He hadn't seen Turner yet or his wife, Claudia. As everyone sang, he thought of *Rock of Ages* as the rocks that the inmates used to have to beat into gravel. The song jogged his memory of the pastor's name—Rickie Tickie. He hoped Rickie, the con man, wouldn't get in the way.

When they finished the song, they started another. Most of the people if not all were over sixty. He was one of the four youngest people he saw and realized now that he stuck out like a kid in an old folks' home. In the middle of the song a couple came in and sat next to him. The woman moved slow and was overweight. He looked at the man next to her and it was Scott Turner, looking rather sharp. The old looking biddy had to be Claudia Turner, he hoped. When they all sat, Baer moved slightly away. The reverend looked at Baer and said, "Welcome to our service, Mister…"

"Lloyd George."

"I hope you will become a member, Mr. George."

"I'm just passing through and thought I'd like to praise the Lord before I left for the road."

"He will be pleased and he will keep you safe, I pray."

"Amen." Someone shouted. Then others joined in.

The reverend began speaking, "For my topic today I will speak about the love Jesus has for all of us, even though we are sinners. Sinners! Maybe not like child predators or rapists but sinners all the same."

"Amen." Most everyone replied.

Baer just couldn't get a good bead on Turner from where he sat and Claudia kept glancing at him smiling. That and the preaching was excruciating to him because the topic was apropos to his visit. He wanted to observe how Turner reacted to the sermon. Baer didn't have a chance. The old biddy kept glancing his way. After the service he couldn't get out quick enough with Claudia moving slow in front of him.

A tap on the shoulder made him turn.

"Glad you picked our church Mister George. I hope it was inspiring."

"Oh, it was, Reverend."

"I had to talk about the plight women have today with predators. No one's safe anymore."

"I know what you mean. And teenage date rape is just as bad today as it was in nineteen sixty-five." Baer hoped Turner was listening.

Smiling Pastor Rickie said, "You're not that old Mister George."

"No, but I've heard stories. Oh, call me Lloyd."

Turner had heard the conversation and it felt like the hand of the Lord slapped him up side of his head. Now Claudia was pestering her husband about inviting the new man for supper. What's wrong with her?

"Where are you from, if you don't mind my asking," Pastor Rickie asked.

Actually, I do mind. "California. San Diego."

"Beautiful part of the country."

Baer looked at his watch. "I'd love to talk but I have a plane to catch."

Claudia poked Turner in the side. He felt like slapping her.

"Go ahead," she said.

Turner frowned at Claudia, then turned on a smile and spoke, "Before you go, my wife and I would love to have you over at the house next time you're in town. Here's our address and phone number."

You're kidding. "Okay. Great. Next time I'm back in town I'll call."

Claudia said, "We'd *love* to have you."

Baer left feeling he'd just been dropped into Bizzarro World. On the flight back maybe he'd have time to think about, what gives? Do they want to convert me? Does she know what he did in High School? Or do they somehow know the other predators are dead? No, too coincidental. Don't believe in coincidences. But none of it makes sense, yet. He hoped Jane won't bother him too much on the flight back. Now he will have to deal with her. *No, you don't,* a voice in his head said. "Shut up," he spoke softly.

On the way back to the house Scott was deep in thought while his wife babbled away.

"Maybe we could convert him. He seems nice. I didn't see a ring. Maybe he's not married. I know just the girl for him."

He wasn't listening, he told her yes, every once in a while. He and the boys—his partners in crime called each other boys—kept in touch. They all still adhered to the pack, that if the law came around, they would deny everything. No witnesses saw what they did to Betty. He remembered her name and she still haunted him. He was the only one who kept his nose clean after that one time for him, but they kept in contact just in case she, Betty, would make trouble. Strange, but last night Jerry Gannon called and said he couldn't get in touch with the others and asked Scott if he heard anything. Seven years ago, he had Jerry take over the task of keeping in touch with everyone each year. Scott thought it was safe enough for Jerry to do the calling, even though sometimes he would also call. Now he thought Jerry was paranoid. Scott told him to check it out. Look at obits. Call the cops.

At the house Turner decided to check also. Maybe something had been going on. He booted up his laptop. He checked The Dundalk Eagle on line and there it was—Clint Zabinski's obit. A short article said, *Mr. Zabinski was shot between the eyes. The police investigated but the case went cold quickly. Police said it looked like a professional hit.* Turner swallowed hard. He checked some more with the *Eagle* and found an article, on a page that said, *News from the Area,* that Kenney Black died of unnatural causes. The police wouldn't elaborate because of ongoing investigation. He noticed there wasn't any mention of the related crime between the two. He couldn't find anything on Jesse Delaney, so he called. No answer. He could be out drinking or drunk, Turner thought. For decades he was nothing but a low life drunk. It's a wonder he hadn't spilled his guts or died of cirrhosis.

He called the bar that he knew Jesse frequented. A bartender answered.

"Yeah, I know Jesse."

"Has he been there lately?"

"He's here usually every day or night, but haven't seen him in a few days."

"If you see him, would you give him this number and call Scott?"

"Yeah. Why not?"

Turner had a sick feeling in his stomach. Did an unknown avenger kill Jesse too? Did Betty finally wake up and hired a hit man? He'd wait a couple of days before he'd start to really worry. But his sixth sense made his spine tingle when something bad was about to happen, and this is the first time it tingled this strong in decades. Why did Mr. George sit in their bench? Heck, what was his first name? Claudia might remember. But he can't let her know anything. He wondered if George was a private dick. Heck the guy had a limp and used a cane. His imagination went wild, then he thought probably it's nothing. They invited him and he looked like he wanted to get away. He'll probably forget about the invite. Yeah, it's nothing.

The tingle stayed strong.

<h1 style="text-align:center">18</h1>

"How did your Florida vacation go?" Smith asked using his landline. Baer was also using his. They both checked for bugs every day.

"It went good. Really too good."

"Oh? Why's that?"

"For some reason they took a shine to me. Probably want to convert me."

Smithe laughed heartily. "Yeah, you need converting."

Baer said nothing.

"Only kidding. What do you think? When will you go back? How much cash do you need?"

"Hold on. One at a time. First off it don't feel right. They've invited me back for a get together the next time I make it to Florida on business."

"That's good."

"No. That's bad. I'm probably gonna have to switch things now and do Gannon next. Get some space before I go back. I was planning next week, but can't now. Too soon. Too risky."

"Whatever you think. This is your forte."

"Let's suppose they kept in touch just in case the law went after them?"

"That would mean they are some kind of gang." Smithe thought that was a good possibility.

"That's what I'm thinking. Turner might be the ring leader. Had the best job, stable life, money, no record. Which means he's damn smart. Or not in the gang."

Smithe was silent.

"Well?"

"Quiet, I'm thinking." After a while Smithe said, "I'll put Lewis and Clark on the idea. Quark will be a great asset."

Baer added, "*If* Turner is the leader, I'll get him last. The others seemed dumber than dog shit and mean. I'll make plans for Gannon. I hope he's dumb too."

"Well, keep in touch," Smithe said.

"Of course."

Turner started to make plans of his own. He signed up with one of the search companies so he could find Betty. He typed in her full maiden name and nothing of value came up. He didn't know her married name so the search site was worthless.

He called a P.I. he was tight with. "Hey, Conrad, I need some P.I. work done."

Conrad Hess was one of the top private investigators in the country. "Meet me at my office at two o'clock, no talking over the phone."

"I'll be there," Turner said.

After all these years someone might be after me, Turner thought. "It's the damn *Me Too* crap," he uttered to himself. *Claudia must never find out, nor the police.*

At Hess's office Turner sweated a bit as he told the P.I. what he wanted. "I need you to check out a man for me. His name is Lloyd George. I think he might be a private investigator like you."

"Why do want to investigate him?"

"I just do!" Turner almost screamed. "I'm sorry Conrad. I haven't had a good day."

"No problem. Where is he from?"

"He said San Diego, California."

"You have any other info on him that might help me?"

Turner looked at his hands. "No."

Hess took a deep breath. "That's not much to go on."

"The impression I got was that he was a "businessman", Turner said, adding air quotes. "That's all I know."

"I'll see what I can find. Keep that dinner invite available and pick his brain. Better yet, invite me too. I'm pretty good at reading people."

"Great idea. I'll let you know when."

Three weeks later Hess called Turner. "Sorry mister X, but I couldn't find any info on your person. Like he never existed. Better invite me to your dinner party."

"Crap. Okay," said Turner. A thousand dollars down the drain. Turner thought that maybe he could take Mr. George down. He was in good shape, for almost seventy-two, and he had some boxing and wrestling experience. *I could probably punch him out.*

Today was the day Baer made plans to scope out Jerry Gannon's house. He hopped into his SUV and left his house in the early morning taking VA. 193 to the D.C. beltway, 495. After some minutes he took exit 33 to Chevy Chase, then headed to Silver Spring. He had the A/C on and music playing from a thumb drive of his favorite music from the sixties and seventies. Baer loved the music though he was not from that generation. He kept in time by tapping the steering wheel as he drove onto MD. 410 and continued to Takoma Park. Took him 50 minutes to get there.

From East-West Highway he made a right onto Clearview Avenue. He found 11069 and drove by slowly. A little way up the street a couple of black kids were out in the street playing catch. He hoped with a rubber ball.

The day had sunshine with puffy white clouds, throwing some shade every now and then. Not much of a breeze. Good for electronics and he brought a directional microphone, since this area would be harder to reconnoiter on foot. The neighborhood wasn't right for walking. That made him use the dash cam and sat it in its spot. He found a place where he could turn around and headed back to Gannon's. He found an open spot two houses from Gannon's, and parked. The day hadn't heated up yet and he kept the windows closed. Inside the car was still cool with the air conditioner off. Baer set up the directional microphone, pointing it at Gannon's house. He placed the headphones on and adjusted the dials to zero in on the house. After a few seconds he could hear sounds inside the house. Then, "Jerry come back to bed."

"I will, baby. I need to wet my whistle."

"I'll wet your whistle," a woman's voice said.

"I'll be there. I'm thirsty." In the upstairs bathroom, Gannon poured himself a shot of Smirnoff in some orange juice and drank. He walked naked back to the bedroom. The floosy held her arms out and the phone rang.

"Don't answer it."

"Got to. Might be a job offer." He knew it wouldn't be.

He picked up the phone by the bed and said "Hello."

She said, "Humph!" and folded her arms under her breasts.

"Doing okay, man. Got my sweetie here."

Baer could only hear one side of the conversation. He didn't bring the two-way directional. His mistake.

Gannon said nothing for a while, then said, "No, shit! When? How?"

Silence. Then, "It's just us two left and the police don't know jack?"

More silence. Baer strained to listen even though he knew it wouldn't do any good.

"Yeah, I'll keep my eyes open. It might all be a coincidence."

Baer smiled.

"Me neither. And don't get pissed off at me. I haven't said a word."

Baer kept smiling.

"You just make sure you keep *your* trap shut, Scott."

Got him, Baer thought. They'll both be in a turmoil now and have their guard up. No problem. He'd use it to his advantage.

"So you think I might be next?"

"Who's that? What's going on, Jerry?" Gannon had the receiver away from his mouth and Baer heard the back feed.

"Shad-up, Glo."

Silence.

"No, she don't know?"

"Know what?"

"Shad-up! Didn't mean to yell in your ear. Hold on."

"Gloria, get dressed and leave. I've got business now to take care of. And this is a private conversation."

Gloria jumped out of bed, got her clothes, hustled down the short hall to the bathroom and slammed the door.

"Okay, she's gone. What am I supposed to do?" Answering to what Scott said. Baer couldn't hear Scott.

"Damned if I know. But I know someone is after us and killing. We're the only two left. You're the only one left in Maryland and it's no coincidence. Shit, be careful. One of us is NEXT." Scott yelled.

"Crap, Scott, quit yelling in my ear. I've got a gun. I'll keep it on me."

"Don't get caught with it. You know Maryland police don't like that."

"Quit your whining. The damn niggers get away with it all the time."

Baer smiled to himself. He wished he could hear Scott.

"In case you haven't noticed, you're not a nigger. They'll come down on you hard."

"Shut up, Scott. You take care of it your way and I'll get his ass my way. Call me back in a month or I'll call you in a month. If we don't hear from each other then, we'll know the other is dead."

His voice trembling Scott said, "Okay," then hung up.

Baer then heard, "Where the hell are you going?" Gannon shouted.

"You told me to leave and I'm leaving, you jackass." She hurried down the stairs and reached the door.

"Get back here! Damn bitch! Damn you Scott, you em eff!" Jerry was riled up.

Baer could only imagine the scene between Gannon and his lover, and his yelling about Turner. Suddenly he saw a well-built beautiful woman with, what else, long flowing blonde hair, storm out of the house. Looking angrier than a wet hen, she bolted to a car, dropped her keys, stomped her foot and finally opened the door. She threw whatever she was carrying across the seat to the passenger side. She jumped in and a few seconds later dashed off, squealing tires. *The neighbors won't like that.* Baer wondered if he should follow her and use her as bait. He thought about the pros and cons in seconds and decided that she would only make things more complicated.

Baer now changed his mind and thought Scott would be next. He was surprised Scott was the one most spooked and more likely to make mistakes. Gannon now seemed tougher and more prepared. Gannon was also one of the few whites in the neighborhood. The neighbors would spot a strange white man quickly. Prince Georges County was one of the wealthiest black counties in Maryland. Besides, it would be good to skip Maryland and do Florida. Might throw the cops off—if they wised up.

Baer left his spot in front of the houses that were close to Jerry's, and headed up the street to a small open area that was used for parking by some of the local residents.

Baer opened the car door and set the drone on the ground. On the ground was less conspicuous when taking off, instead of holding it out the window. After closing the door, he worked the controls and it took off instantly. He hovered over Gannon's house, camera recording so he could look at it back at the Underground. Slowly he circled the drone around the house then brought it back to his car. Opening the car door after it landed, he picked it up and put it back into its small case. He drove to exit the lot when a Prince Georges County Ford Police Interceptor car blocked him and lit up.

Baer thought *crap.* The cop got out and Baer turned off the ignition. He rolled the window down on his SUV. Wearing light blue slacks with a black stripe, the uniformed black officer walked towards him.

"Morning, sir. Got a call someone was loitering here. Would that be you?"

"I didn't see anyone loitering officer."

"Said it was an unfamiliar SUV. Yours?"

"Could be, sir. I used to live here and I was just sitting reminiscing."

"No harm in that. Could I see your driver's license and registration?"

"Sure thing." Baer complied.

"Shady Oak, Virginia. Do you have a carry license from Virginia?"

"No, sir. May I ask why someone would call? I thought this was public parking."

"It is, but some people think it's their private parking area."

"I can understand. In this day and age people are more cautious. That's good. Keeps my childhood home safe."

"Sit tight. I'll be back." The Officer walked back to his car. In a few minutes he came back. Handing the license and registration back, the LEO said, "Go ahead and do your reminiscing. I'll let the caller know it's an old homesteader."

Smiling Baer said, "Hey, I'm not that old, officer," and stuck his hand out to shake. The LEO took it.

Baer made a right out of the lot and drove slowly down the slight hill like he was looking at memories. He came to East-West Highway and turned left. He let out a deep breath. Close call but it worked out. Being cautious and polite to Law Enforcement Officers helps a lot to get you on your way quickly. Plus a good fake I.D. One thing he learned; too many eyes watching, so he would have to draw Gannon away from his house—somehow.

Baer, being a freelancer, had managed to dodge all intelligence agencies and kept a very low profile. Being polite to the LEOs was just one means of staying anonymous. Ex-Senator John Smithe kept Baer's back covered all the time. Lewis and Clark also helped keep Baer out of the limelight. The geeks also had an ace up their sleeves. They had their moles working in the NSA—their brothers, Holmes and Watson.

19

Smithe called Witkowski. "Hey, Witty, this is John. I have another update for our client."

"Great. I'll pass it on."

"So far three out of five have been eliminated from this life. No complications. But it appears the last two will take a little longer and more planning. One of them is out of state. I think you can let him know this. One is in Florida, and one is in Maryland. The rest were and are dead in Maryland."

"No problem. I'll tell the go between and he'll get the funds and I'll send it to you."

"When this is over, we'll give your client the high school pictures and their mug shots…at no extra charge." Smithe chuckled.

"Personally, I think he would like that."

"So, how are you?"

"This Covid bull crap is cramping my style, senator, but we're doing good. Tessa keeps me on the go. It's still pretty good here in Florida."

"You're lucky to have her."

"I know."

"Tell her I said, hi."

CHAPTER 19

"Will do."

"Talk to you later." The senator hung up.

Witkowski called Lance Pruitt. "Lance, tell your person, three down, two to go but will take longer because one lives in Florida. And get some money so I can send it off."

"Will do, Nick. He'll be pleased with the news."

"Also, he'll send photos and mug shots."

"I'll pass that on."

They hung up. No chit chat. Lance dialed Karl Kephart's number. Betty answered.

"This is Lance, Betty. Is your old cowboy around?"

"Yes. I'll go get him."

Lance knew she doesn't know what's happening and that's the way Karl wanted it.

"Lance, me boy. How goes it?"

"Great. Just got the word. Three down, two to go."

"Wonderful. When this is over, I'd like a written report. No names of the cleaner or cleaners. Just how it was done. Get my monies worth. Then I'll burn it. Verstehen?"

"Yes, I understand. They will also give you high school photos and mug shots. They also asked for funds to complete it. The last two clean ups will take longer because one lives in Florida and that's more time consuming."

"Come on over and I'll give you three thousand in used currency, to give to your guy. And I do want the photos."

"I'll be right over." Lance would deposit the money into his checking account that he used for wire transfers. Used cash hardly raises any red flags. New currency might, because of the drug dealers. But they sometimes mix it up with used money.

Next he called Nick. "I'm going to pick up the cash now. Where do you want to meet?" Lance asked.

"I live in Florida or have you forgotten?"

"Yeah, I know. I forgot." Then in a very low tone, "Angie just walked by—naked. Threw me off."

Laughing, Nick said, "You're forgiven."

"Well, I best be on my way to pick it up and I'll wire it to you as usual."

"Go now and no hanky-panky before you leave." Witkowski laughed again.

"I'll get it as soon as I can. Maybe forty-five minutes before I leave."

"Okay, okay. Bye."

An hour and a half later, Nick had the money. Ten minutes later, Nick wired it to Smithe.

20

Baer sat in his usual chair in the Smithe's den. Smithe leaned forward slightly and Baer stretched out to reach the money. Baer pocketed it without looking or counting it. Like father to son.

"Fifteen hundred enough for both jobs?" Smithe asked.

"Should be. If I need more, I know who to go to," Baer said smiling.

Jeeves walked in. "Drinks, sir?"

"Yes, please. Same as usual."

"Very good, sir." He left.

Baer said, "I called Scott and his wife answered. Told her I'd be in town next week. She was thrilled."

Smithe raised his eyebrows. "She's not going to try to put the make on you, is she?"

"Nein. She's just a nice person. Too bad she's going to be a widow soon," he scoffed.

"Yeah, breaks my heart," Smithe scowled.

"Besides, remember that old Arthur Godfrey song?"

Smithe look at him quizzically, "Which one?"

Baer started to sing, "Oh, I don't want her you can have her…"

"…she's too fat for me." Smithe finished.

They both were laughing as Jeeves walked in and gave each one their drinks, Smithe first.

"Anything else, sir?"

"No, thanks, Jeeves," Smith chuckled.

Jeeves bowed slightly and left. Baer still had a slight grin on his face.

"What?" Smithe asked. "You said she was fat."

"Not that. I'm not used to a butler."

Ignoring the remark and getting back to business, Smithe asked, "How are you going to plan Scott's demise?"

"Don't know yet. I plan as I go along. Besides, you don't want to know."

"I know the papers don't know anything except the cases are going cold."

"Good. That's the way it should be." He hadn't told Smithe about Jane Stafford yet. She was always on his mind. He didn't want to screw things up, but she was a powerful, pulling, distraction. And he knew distractions could get you killed.

Baer flew Delta this time into Southwestern Florida International Airport, arriving at Concourse C. He had been tempted to use Southwest but he didn't want the complication. Later he would seek her out.

Had to wear a mask again during the flight and for his line of work he hoped the idiots—so called leaders, would keep the mask "Mandate" going. This time he brought his own miniatures to drink and peanuts to eat, with some bee pollen. There was nothing else the airlines or politicians could do to make flying more unenjoyable because of the phony Covid-19 Pandemic. Well, maybe they could by having no flight attendants. Just security mask enforcers. Damn communists.

He knew the man-made virus was real, and Baer had a knack for turning sour grapes into wine.

Baer had called Turner's house the day before he left for Florida. He wanted to make sure everything was a go. It was and Scott Turner offered to pick him up. Baer had said no thanks. This was a business trip and the business would pay for the ride. Turner had actually sounded disappointed. Wonder why?

His Buddy Robert Rocke, a former Navy SEAL, who had helped him eliminate the illegal alien murderer in California, lived in north Fort Myers and had all the accoutrements he needed for the job. He would have to be paid in cash. No questions asked, no answers given. Rocke lived in Lazy Days Village. Last house on dead end Sundown St., off of Easy St. Baer could tell it was a retirement area. Great idea for a place to hide in plain sight.

Baer parked the rental in the driveway and walked up to the door and knocked. The door opened.

"Hey, double R, nice digs you have here," Baer used his nickname.

"I have to admit, it's a perfect fit, except for this damn beard I have to dye every five days."

"Yeah, an old guy with a *white* beard and no hair wouldn't look right," Baer chuckled.

"No older than you. Nice to see you, too."

They hugged and back slapped each other.

"I'm too damn young to have a gray beard…or hair, what's left of it."

"If you say so," Baer quipped.

"Follow me," double R said. He led Baer to a small room. He switched on a light switch and then another switch which opened a small portion of the wall to reveal a larger room filled with guns hanging on the wall, ammo and explosives sitting on the floor, small gold & silver bars on a shelf, and a plethora of knives in a cabinet.

"Man, I need this type of room." Baer was thoroughly impressed.

"Whatever you need man, I've got."

While Baer looked around, he said, "I need sodium pentothal, syringe, a mesh mask and a tape recorder or some facsimile thereof. Also, a hand-held voice modulator."

"The mesh mask and tape recorder are on the shelf over there." Rocke pointed. "The other stuff is in my floor safe." Rocke felt along the floor, pushed a small fake metal board down which made its long end swing up on a hinge. He grabbed it and pulled up. In the 12-inch-long by 4-inch-wide by 6-inch-deep safe, he reached in and pulled all the items out one by one.

"Damn, what a set-up," Baer remarked.

Rocke smiled. "All of this is fresh, never been used. I always replace stuff I use with new stuff."

"Man, you Navy Seals have got it."

"I'm RED, man."

"I know you're retired, and now I know you are extremely dangerous. Glad you're on my side, double R."

"Between you and me, I'm waiting for a clandestine wet work now," Rocke volunteered.

"As you probably guessed, I'm doing some now."

"Of course, we're in the same brotherhood. Nice to talk to a patriot in the know. The senator is a great man."

"That he is," Baer agreed. "He's my step dad."

Rocke walked up to him and bear hugged him again. "Come into the kitchen, we'll have a couple of beers and shoot the shit."

"Sounds great." Baer followed him and they drank. And they talked.

The next day he made it, in time, to the 9:30 service at the church driving the rental. Rocke, in his Ford Expedition, sat outside the church waiting for Baer.

Baer was to follow Turner to his house and Rocke was to follow them. Baer had the same disguise he wore when he first met Turner. Rocke was disguised also.

After the services, Baer went into Turner's house. Rocke left and drove to his house. Later Baer would drive Turner to Rocke's place. They wanted to make sure Turner left his car.

To Baer's surprise Conrad Hess arrived two minutes later.

"Lloyd, I like you to meet a friend of mine, Conrad Hess."

"My pleasure to finally meet you Mr. George. Scott has told me you're a businessman?"

"Yes."

"What type of business, Mr. George?"

"Import/Export type, Mr. Hess." Right away Baer didn't like him. This clown is fishing. Must be the private eye Smithe had given him a heads up on. "What type of business are you in, Mr. Hess?"

"Treasure Hunting. Finding lost objects." Hess smiled. *Like people. You're not James Bond. Import/Export my foot.*

"Find any treasures lately?" Baer baited him.

"Actually, yes, but I need to find where it came from." Hess kept smiling.

Baer smiled back. "I'm sure you'll find out."

"Yes, yes, I will."

Claudia called, "Dinner's ready gentlemen."

When dinner was over Baer said he'd like Turner to look at some property—which would be Rocke's house. He told Turner that he was thinking about moving to Florida because of the taxes and weather. Today had a few clouds and bright sunshine. Temperature was a perfect 81 degrees, light breeze. California was getting too liberal and raising taxes. Plus they had a prima donna dictator for a governor.

Turner thought that was terrific. Better living conditions. Hess had asked Mr. George questions that he couldn't bring up. The way Lloyd talked—he was not here to kill him. He had the guy pegged wrong.

After dinner they all walked outside and Baer said goodbye to Mrs. Turner and Hess. Hess walked slowly to his car.

Baer kept an eye on the rear-view mirror but didn't see Hess follow, though he never saw what car Hess drove. He drove through the development then back tracked down another street. When he was satisfied they weren't being followed, he finally reached Rocke's house. They left Baer's car and knocked on the door and Rocke made like a salesperson. Robert Rocke wore a sport coat for the ruse and started to show the house. The coat covered a holstered Colt .45. Rocke excused himself and told them to look on their own. They started to look around the bedroom.

Turner finally spoke, "This is a nice small house. Just right for a single guy."

Rocke had gone to the kitchen, opened a drawer and took out a chloroform patch in its envelope. On his way to the bedroom Rocke ripped open the chloroform envelope. He carried it to the bedroom the other two were in. Turner didn't hear Rocke approach. Baer distracted Turner by saying, "Look at this. I think you're right, Mister Turner."

From behind Rocke grabbed Turner and covered his mouth and nose with the patch. Gently he followed Turner to the floor. With Turner knocked out they lifted him and dropped him onto the bed. "I'll get a dinette chair," Rocke said.

They placed him on the chair and ducted taped his legs to the back legs of the chair. Baer then duct taped Turner's hands behind him. He finished taping Turner's body to the chair when he started stirring. Baer quickly put tape across his eyes. The plan was Baer would ask the prearranged questions using the voice modulator.

"Wha happen?" Turner slurred. "I can't see."

Baer slapped him across the face. Baer's modulated voice said, "Shut up. I'll ask the questions."

Baer had put on Rocke's robe and pulled the mesh mask down over his face. Rocke had sprayed some floral aerosol to hide any smells. Rocke busied himself cutting away Turner's shirt sleeve at the bicep. Then he pulled it down to the wrist, bunched up. Rocke placed a tourniquet and tightened it slightly above Turner's bicep to make the veins stand out better. He stood behind the rapist.

Baer ripped the tape off Turner's eyes. "Ow!" He blinked. "Wha…the hell. Who are you? What you want?" Turner was coming out of the chloroform.

"I said shut up!" Rocke disguised his voice in a deep baritone.

Turner tried to look behind him, that's where the voice came from—he was sure. Then he looked at Baer. "Who are you? What do you want? What's going on? I have money. Let me go and I'll give…"

"Shut up!" the voice behind him said again. They were double teaming Turner to confuse and to disorient him.

Turner was scared shitless but managed some courage to say, "Cut me loose and I'll give you ten thousand dollars. I promise I won't say anything to anybody."

"My, such a tempting bribe from a tied-up piece of shit rapist." The baritone voice came from behind him again.

"Who're you?" Turner tried again to look behind him but couldn't. Now he was really afraid for his life. He whimpered, "What do you want?"

Baer looked at him. "I'm going to get your confession."

"What am I suppose to confess? What do you want to hear?"

"The truth. Did you rape Elizabeth Crenshaw in nineteen sixty-five?"

"Elizabeth who? Never heard of her."

"Wrong answer, rapist." Baer grabbed the vial labeled sodium pentothal, tilted it upside down and stuck the tip of the syringe through the rubber top. Pulling the plunger back, he filled it halfway. After putting the truth serum back in the case, he let the bubbles rise to the top of the syringe and squeezed some of the fluid out.

Scott Turner had watched but couldn't believe what was going on. "What are you doing?"

Baer found a good bulging blue vein, poked the needle in and depressed the plunger. Waiting for the drug to take effect, he set up the tape recorder, video camera, and set of small speakers.

No iPhone for this. Just destroy the tape and chip or send them to the cops. No footprint.

Drug would take effect around 8 to10 minutes.

Bear held the voice modulator in his left hand and the microphone in his right hand.

"Any chance he'll lie?" said a whispered voice behind Turner.

"No, I've used it before and you can't fight it," the modulated voice said behind the mesh mask.

"I'll give you fourteen thousand and never say a word," pleaded Turner.

"For what you did, shithead, a million wouldn't be enough, "Baer's modulated voice said.

Turner dropped his head and said, "That's all I have."

Ten minutes later, Baer stepped away from Turner out of camera range. He turned the camera and tape recorder on. He held the recorder's microphone to Turner's mouth. Speaking into modulator Baer asked, "What is your name?"

"Scott Turner."

"Any middle name?"

"No."

Where do you live?"

"Four four two five Rotary Circle.

"What State?"

"Florida."

"Any children?"

"No."

"Where did you grow up?"

"Dundalk, Maryland."

"What high school did you go to?"

"Dundalk Senior High School."

"Go Owl's," Baer said sarcastically.

"You went there?" Turner asked.

"I'll ask the questions."

Baer was establishing the background so any investigator would know exactly who he was. He also had Turner give his past job history and where he lived in Dundalk, as well as the Florida telephone numbers.

With Turner's identity established Baer went on to the crime.

"Scott. Can I call you Scott?" Baer asked to establish an even tighter relationship with the drugged scumbag.

"Yes."

"Scott, do you remember a night in nineteen sixty-five when you raped a classmate named Betty Crenshaw?"

"I remember a Betty. Didn't know her last name. But no one cared."

"By no one, who do you mean.?"

"Me and the other guys." Scott had a grin that grew wider as he spoke. "Man. She was hot. I got her first. We all laid her. What a night."

"Who were the other guys with you?"

"Yeah, we all got her. She just laid there."

"Scott, just answer my questions. What were the names of the others?"

Turner furrowed his brow. "Um, Jesse somebody, who drove and gave us the wine."

"Jesse Delaney?"

"I guess that could have been his name. Don't really remember."

"Scott, don't lie to me."

"Yeh, Jesse Delaney."

"Who else?" Baer needed all of the names to make the case, so to speak. He wanted to be thorough.

"Clint Zabinski, um, Jerry Gannon, ah, me. That's it. Four of us. That's all that could fit in the Super Sport. Had to leave Kenny Black behind." Turner chuckled, "Poor guy was pissed."

"Have you kept track of them through the years?"

"Yeah, we made a pact to keep our mouths shut."

"Did they?"

"I think so. But lately they've been dying or killed."

"Why do you think that?"

"Because I called them, or Jerry Gannon, about every eight months and some didn't answer and I'd seen obits for two of them"

"So, all of you had a good time with Betty? You, Jesse, Clint and Jerry?"

"Oh yes."

"What would your wife think?"

"She'd kill me. Don't tell her." He looked scared. Really scared.

"I won't Scott but I have a message from Betty's husband."

"Her husband?"

"Yes, and he just found out what you did and he's very, very, angry."

"Shit, he could tell my wife."

"He could but *he* won't"

Rocke was smiling behind Turner as he watched Baer.

"Why not?"

"Cause he wants you strung up by the balls."

Rocke's laughter sounded weird coming through his hand.

"But she had it coming. Drunk and all that."

Baer stopped the recording.

Rocke slapped the back of Turner's head.

"Hey, who did that!" Turner yelled. "Damn, I knew I should have had a hidey hole like Jerry."

Baer stared at Scott and said, "What do you mean?"

"Jerry has a cousin in eastern West Virginia. Lives in a small cabin. No one around. We talked about going there to check it out in case something like this happened."

"You mean like you dying?"

"I didn't say anything about dying."

Baer put the modulator down. "You know Turner, you're a big piece of shit." Baer spat the words.

Baer grabbed the empty syringe, pulled the plunger back, filling it with air, while Turner watched. "Now I recognize your voice. It's you! Lloyd! Gonna give me more of that stuff? You can't. It's empty." He started to breathe heavy, taking in gulps of air.

Baer took off the mask. "You piece of dog shit." Baer began, "I will kill you with this, only it will take a few minutes but you'll know you're dying. Just like you knew when you were rapping Betty. And your wife will know what you did."

"You can't do this. It's inhuman." Scott tried to move and Rocke held him still.

With utter disdain Baer stabbed the needle into Scott's arm and depressed the plunger, sending thousands of lethal air bubbles into Turner's bloodstream. He didn't want to watch or hear him die so he told Rocke to get a blanket to wrap the rapist in. They'll use it for disposal. As Rocke went to get a blanket in the closet there was a knock at the door, Baer froze and listened. Police? Wife? Pastor? Salesman? P.I.? Baer went for the tape and taped Turner's mouth. Then he grabbed the blanket from Rocke and threw it hap-hazard on the dying rapist.

Robert Rocke walked to the door and opened it a crack. "Yes. What do you want?'

"Hi, sir. My name is Conrad Hess. I'm looking for Scott Turner. He called me earlier and said he'd be here."

Rocke thought quick, *this guy is full of shit. Should I pull him in or blow him off?* He chose.

"No one lives here by that name. You got the wrong address."

Rocke started to shut the door but Hess's foot stopped it.

"Sorry, but the address is right."

Baer heard what was going on from the hall around the corner. The name Hess sounded familiar. With Turner's body in the bedroom, he closed the bedroom door. Baer walked in. "Who's that, double R?"

"Rudolf Hess, looking for a guy named Turner."

Conrad Hess pushed past Rocke. "Oh, it's you. He said he'd be here, Mister George."

"That's a lie, Conrad. Turner didn't know the address." Baer stared at him. "You bugged my car. I'm slipping Bob. I should have checked."

Rocke growled, "Rudolf you shouldn't have done that."

Hess squinted at Rocke. "You I don't like. I know what you're trying to do by calling me Rudolf. It worked. I won't deal with you."

Rocke laughed.

Hess turned back to Baer. "Come now Mister George, let's do this right." Hess said and put out his hand.

Rocke went over to the front door and locked it.

Hess tried to give Baer a bone crusher shake but Baer had his thumb in his palm. "That's not cute, Hess."

Hess let go.

Baer said, "Hess here is a private dick, looking for Turner. Well dick, he's not here."

"Hess dropped his voice, "Cut the crap, George, or whatever your name is. I saw him come in."

"So you did follow us." Baer said.

"You're right, I put a bug on your car," he chuckled.

Rocke was behind Hess, moving closer.

"Back off, big guy." Hess turned his head slightly and his tone changed. "I don't play games but I do have an offer." Now Hess turned so he could see both, Baer on his right and Rocke on his left. "We could play tough guy but then my offer is off."

Baer said, "I know you think you're still a tough Ranger."

"You've checked on me. Good. My job now is making money, lots of it. I have no use for Turner and I don't care where you put him. I couldn't find you Lloyd. You're invisible. Congrats."

"What do you want," Rocke said.

Still looking at Baer he said, "I told you, Mister Lloyd, Money. Lots."

Baer was running options through his head but nothing good came up. "So, we give you lots of money and you just disappear?"

"That's the gist of it."

Rocke caught Baer's eye and frowned.

Baer said, "Hess, we don't have that kind of money. That's not how we operate."

Baer had no idea how to get out of this mess. Yes, Hess was a mess. He raised his eyebrows to Rocke, it was his house.

Rocke said, "Get out of my house."

Hess raised his hands in surrender. "Okay, if that's the way you want it." He turned towards the door to leave. "No hard feelings," he said, as he was about to unlock the door and walk out.

"Wait, Hess," Rocke said.

Hess stopped and turned around. The blast from Rocke's Colt .45 made Baer jump as Hess fell backwards into the door.

"Damn, Bob, I didn't see that coming."

"Neither did he," Rocke smiled. "Hope the old folks around here are deaf."

"Did the round go through the door?"

"Naw. I'm using special fragmentators."

"Now we got two stiffs to get rid of."

"Not a problem. We'll back my car into the garage, put 'em in the trunk, drive to the Paradise Marina, put 'em on my boat, weigh 'em down and dump 'em for shark bait."

"Sounds good to me. Let's get started."

They laid both men on tarps on the floor. They stripped the clothes off of them. Double R got some acid from one of his selves. He poured the acid in a bowl and Baer held the bowl while Rocke dipped the fingers into the bowl to burn off the fingerprints and then some. After that Rocke went to work pulling, twisting, yanking their teeth out with large pliers. Perspiration dripped from him. Then they wrapped the bodies in blankets and duct tape them. They carefully tossed them in the trunk, so as not to make any noise. Bob Rocke threw some garden edging blocks in for weights. Double R grabbed more duct tape and tossed it in also.

"Damn that was a lot of work," Baer said wiping the sweat off his forehead with a hand.

"Yeah, but it's safer with no teeth and no prints...just in case."

Baer knew what he meant.

"Let's go," Rocke said.

Rocke took U.S. 41 south to get to the marina.

Once on the boat Rocke headed out to sea. At the seven-mile spot Rocke cut the engines. They took the bodies out of the blankets and using plenty of duct tape they wrapped the blocks to the bodies. When finished, Baer grabbed the upper body and Rocke had the feet and they swung each overboard.

Rocke started the engines and they headed back, in the twilight, lights out.

When they got back, they made three copies of the cassette tape and three copies of the video chip. Rocke kept a set. Baer kept one set and handed the third set to Rocke. "Delete the names he gave us, then make a new copy and give that copy to his wife. Give me more time for a get-a-way. It'll take longer to get to the right authorities."

"Those were my plans. Ahead of you, brotherman." He smiled.

"Send that other set with all the info to the senator. That way you are clean."

"Will do."

When finished they hugged and slapped each other on the back. Then Baer reached into his secret pocket and said, "Here's the fifteen hundred dollars for helping."

"Great, my friend. Let me know whenever you need me again."

"Of course. Now let's get rid of Hess's car," Baer said.

After Baer found the bug on the rental, he gave it to Rocke. Rocke got into Hess's car and Baer followed to a small shopping center. Rocke parked it in the middle of the packed lot. Rocke knew the parking lot was not surveilled by cameras and no others were nearby. After he wiped the car down, he jumped into Baer's rental.

Baer drove Rocke back to his house and left in the rental. He drove the rental to his motel to wait until he was scheduled to fly out. He packed the tape and video in a special compartment in his one-piece luggage. He would make other copies later at home—just in case.

Baer got to the motel, threw off his clothes, and took one of the miniatures. He went to a soda machine they had outside and got a 7-up. When he got back to his room, he called the senator.

"You'll be getting a package in the mail soon. Put it in the safe."

"I will. So it went well?"

"Very well. No problems." No details over the phone. Smithe didn't want to hear the details anyway.

"Great. Goodnight, son."

"Goodnight, pops."

Smithe was about to say something but Baer had already hung up on him.

After finishing his nightcap and super tired, Baer collapsed onto the bed and set the alarm for 5 A.M. and promptly fell asleep.

The next day Claudia Turner received the cassette tape and a recorder/play-back machine via a private special messenger. Both were wiped clean. It said: From Scott. She had wondered where Scott was. She immediately listened to it. Shocked and furious at what she heard, she immediately ripped the tape apart and smashed it. She threw the playback machine on the floor and stomped it. Then she grabbed her chest.

21

Baer decided to change his flight from Delta to Southwest in the hope he'd get an earlier flight to Dulles. When he called the airlines, things worked out perfectly. His luck was holding out. Southwest had a flight leaving at 7 A.M. His main reason for changing was that he hoped to stay lucky and see Jane Stafford. A long shot, but he took it, not knowing her schedule. He was greeted by a different woman attendant. He was fortunate enough to get a seat across from where he sat before.

Baer looked around when he boarded but didn't see her. Disappointed, he took his seat and settled in.

Shortly he felt a tap on his shoulder and a woman's voice said, "Excuse me, sir, would you mind getting up and let this lady and gentleman get to their seats?"

A voice he remembered. He got up, looked and smiled. "Jane. My pleasure." He grabbed his cane, leaning on it as he stepped in the aisle. "Go ahead, ma'am; sir."

They went to their seats and Baer stood watching Jane, as she helped the couple settle in.

He had a schoolboy grin on his face when Jane turned towards him.

She smiled and said, "Long time no see. I guess your business is over and heading back to Dulles?"

"Yes, to both. Do you have a layover in Dee Cee when we get there?"

"Yes. Why?"

"I thought maybe, if you're not busy, we could go to a restaurant in Georgetown, have dinner and drinks."

Before she could answer, the second flight attendant "paged" her by yelling, "Jane! Come quickly."

"Excuse me. I'll be right back." She moved along the aisle quick and smooth. "What's the matter?" Jane asked when she reached the attendant.

"Mister Bowley, doesn't want to buckle his seat belt." The man sat in the middle seat.

"We're not moving. I'll buckle it when we're moving!" One could tell, even with the mask on, Bowley made a face.

Jane leaned over and said, "Sir, we all have to buckle up now before we move so the pilot doesn't have to have another worry."

"Worry? What's he have to worry about? Is there a bomb on board?!"

The passengers started mumbling.

"No sir. It's standard procedure. Is this your first flight?"

"Yes. And I want to get off if there's a bomb."

Someone close said, "Bomb?"

Baer heard that in the back row. He could see and sense the other passengers were going to riot, so to speak, if he didn't step in.

He left his seat and headed quickly toward the trouble, limping. Jane was leaning over with her hand on the man's shoulder trying to calm him. "Get your hand off me!" and slapped her hand away. Jane stood and asked the seated aisle passenger to step into the aisle a moment. He did. By that time Baer was right there. He gently moved Jane and the man down the aisle a foot, while the other female attendant moved toward the cockpit, then stopped.

Baer sat in the empty seat. He turned to the man and reached around and hooked his arm around the man's neck. The man said, "Wha…" as Baer brought the man's head and ear close to his masked mouth. He spoke low and harsh, "Listen, dip-shit, buckle your damn belt, behave yourself or I'll rip your ear off with my teeth. Understand?"

The man squeaked out, "yes." Baer let go and shoved him back. The man nervously buckled his belt after two tries. The woman sitting in the window seat next to the first-time flyer, buckled hers quickly on the first try. Baer said to the man, "Keep it buckled." He stood, eyes twinkling over the mask and said to the standing passenger, "You can have your seat back now."

"Thank you." He sat nervously and clicked his belt. At the same time there was a cacophony of belts clicking. Baer limped back to his seat while people stole looks at him, then quickly looked away. Jane walked behind him smiling and looking at the passengers as they snapped their belts. *He's my ABP.*

Baer reached his seat and sat.

She stopped, pulled her mask down, smiled and looked at Jake. "Now you buckle your belt, sir."

"Yes, ma'am." Click. He had smiled back but his mask was up.

"I'll stop by after takeoff, about the offer." She walked toward the galley where she took her seat.

Over the loudspeaker the pilot spoke. "Ladies and gentlemen, we are now on the taxi-way, proceeding to the runway for departure. It will take a few minutes as we will be in a queue. Thank you."

In flight, after Jane finished her duties with her group of passengers she stopped by Baer's seat.

"So, you were saying?"

"Yes. Jane, Stafford, right?"

"Yes. You're Lloyd George, right?" She had read the passenger manifest.

"Yes, and I know of a nice restaurant in Georgetown I'd like to invite you to have dinner with me."

"Well, that's a nice sentence, so I'll say yes. But I want to go home first and freshen up and change into something nice."

Baer smiled. "You don't have to change. I like you the way you are."

"Okay, I can take that two ways. So, I'll be specific. I want to wash up and change my clothes."

"As long as you're the same person when we go out." He chuckled.

"So…you're a cut-up."

"Guilty, ma'am."

"I like that. I noticed you can be serious too. Like with that passenger."

"You bet. I have a way with words."

They both laughed. Then she said, "Later. I'm still working."

"I don't mind watching you work."

She slapped him on the arm and went up the aisle to see if anyone needed anything, some water or a pillow. That was all the passengers were allowed. After that she went back to her seat, winked at Baer when she passed him.

Baer checked into a quaint establishment called the Georgetown House on 31st Street N.W. Once settled in, he showered, put on a fresh suit and tie, then called Smithe on the scrambler.

"So it went well with Scott, I assume," Smithe said.

"Pretty much. There was one glitch we had to take care of at the same time. No biggie. Some P.I. that thought he could play the big leagues."

"Don't want to hear anymore. Is there an extra fee for that?"

"No. Came with the package. Details later. I've got a date. Bye."

Smithe looked at the phone and shook his head. Well, that assignment was over and letting your hair down helped ease the tension. Ah, to be young again.

Jake Baer picked up Jane Stafford at the prearranged time. Luck was with him a third time and he found a parking spot in front of her 10-story apartment building at the 1330 Apartments on 7th Street N.W. He sat and waited for her in his rented Ford SUV. In two minutes, she knocked on the window, he unlocked the door and she hopped in, smelling of orchids.

"Hi," she greeted.

"You smell good," he answered. He pulled away from the curb.

"What place did you pick, Lloyd?"

"The 1789 Restaurant on 36th street."

"I've never been there. "

"Me neither, so it's going to be interesting. Someone told me it was an excellent place with a great atmosphere. Won't take long to get there."

"Good. I'm starving."

In the restaurant, Jane was busy looking around as they were led to a table in one of the rooms that had many pictures of different scenes and sizes, filling every available space on the walls.

When they were seated Jane remarked, "This reminds me a little bit of Haussner's in Baltimore."

Jake/Lloyd said, "I thought they closed down."

"It is. Really sad. I miss it."

"What closed it?"

"Death in the family. It was family owned."

"At least this place is alive."

She chuckled.

They weren't wearing masks. Hardly anyone wore a mask. *Must be Republicans,* Baer thought.

The menus came and they ordered. Baer ordered two glasses of Prosecco Extra Dry Superiore Valdobbiadene, Italian wine at $10 a glass. He also ordered for both and she agreed with his choice, Rebuli with Salmon Crudo. Expensive but she was worth it. He also wanted to make a good impression. And it worked.

Before he took her to his hotel, he asked her if she wanted to stop by his hotel for a night cap. She said yes—of course.

When they entered the hotel, she remarked that it was nice and quaint.

"You noticed that too."

She slapped his arm, smiling.

In the room he fixed two vodka tonics and handed one to her. He sipped his and she downed hers quickly.

"Boy was I thirsty. Fix me another, please."

"Sure thing." He grinned as he fixed it and knew the drinks would relax her. But he didn't want her drunk.

He handed her the drink and said, "Drink a little slower, okay?"

"Okay." She downed half of it. "This is good. Especially after a wonderful dinner. Thank you."

"My pleasure, Janie."

"Oh, you're so sweet. My close friends call me Janie."

"I'll give you the grand tour. You're in the living room, quite small as you noticed."

She giggled. He was a mystery man to her. She liked that. She wanted to unlock the mystery.

"Next, we have the bedroom with a double size bed. Small also."

"If you had someone in there with you, it would be cozy."

"Yes it would. "

She plopped on the bed almost spilling her drink. "Whoops." She threw her head back and laughed.

"You have a wonderful laugh."

"Thanks." Her short white skirt had ridden halfway up her legs. "So where in Alexandria do you live?"

"Actually, I live a little west of Alexandria since I'm stationed now in America. The United States is a member of Interpol. Interpol has satellite offices around the world."

"I didn't know that," she said as she finished her drink. "How far west of Alexandria do you live?"

"Not too far. In Shady Oaks."

"I bet it's shady there," she laughed.

"Yes it is, and private, you lovely cornball."

"It's private in here. Why don't you sit next to me?"

He sat and she grabbed him and kissed him on the lips passionately. It didn't take them long before both were undressed and made love.

After the exercise they rested and laid on their sides facing each other, making small talk. Then they made love again, slowly and methodically. When finished they fell asleep in each other's arms.

Baer's alarm rang at seven. He woke with a start and quickly got his bearings when he looked at Jane waking and stretching. The sheet lay across her flat belly. Smiling, he propped himself on his elbow and watched her as she awakened.

"Good morning," he said.

She looked over and saw him, jerked slightly and said, "Oh!" She raised her head slightly. "Now I know where I am," she smiled. She hadn't bother to cover herself.

"Sleep well?" he asked.

"Very. Why don't we freshen up and make love again before I have to go?"

"Your wish is my command."

"After I finish this job I'm on, I'll invite you to my house," Jake said. He hadn't told her his real name yet. Too early.

"Good. I have some vacation days coming."

"Here, I'll give you my phone number, just in case. If I don't answer, which I probably won't, I'm gone a lot, leave a message. I'll get back to you."

"Thanks, sweetie," she giggled.

"I like you a lot, Jane. Just letting you know."

"I like you very much, sweetie. Just letting you know." She smiled.

Baer didn't know what to say.

"Did I scare you, Hon?" Jane asked.

"No. Just happily surprised."

They hugged and kissed. "I hate to let you go, Lloyd." Jane made a sad face.

"Me too. One day I'll tell you all about myself."

They hugged again.

They made it back to her place just in time for her to change and go to Dulles for today's schedule. He kissed her goodbye and drove to Shady Oaks.

Baer couldn't get her out of his mind. Would it be possible to marry her and still do what he does? He'd never survive a 9-5 job, if those jobs still existed. His jobs could be a problem and put a wife in harm's way. If, and that's a big if, if he married her, how could he protect her from his enemies? It would have to be a secret marriage and no one would be able to know that he had a wife—except the senator. He wondered if that was a real possibility, to be married and hide her in plain sight, maybe as a secretary for *Home Restorations* or something like that. He'd have to sleep on it.

22

When Baer arrived home, he immediately called Smithe on the landline and told him some of the details about Turner biting the dust.

"Okay, I get the picture. I don't need to know more, except, what took you so long? I thought you'd be back yesterday. Have any trouble?"

"No. No trouble. Unless you call meeting a lady friend and spending the night with her, trouble."

"What? In your disguise?"

"Yes and it wasn't a problem. Though I was a little worried about the hair, but it held on." He chuckled.

"Lady friend, my ass. You have time for that? What about your cover?"

"Everything's cool, John. No worries."

"Let's hope not. Where did you meet her?"

"On the plane to and from Florida."

"Great scot, man, what the hell is the matter with you? Belay that remark. What does she do for a living?"

"She's a Southwest Airlines flight attendant, and pretty."

"Great Caesar's ghost. Another one? I hope she'll be better for you than Heidi was."

"I'll find out, won't I." Baer laughed. "She's great, Perry White."

"Okay, okay. While I have you on the phone, I sent a trusted friend to scout for property in eastern Oklahoma. My house is on the market and I'm moving ASAP."

Baer was taken aback. "Okay. Then I'm putting mine up for sale, too. Virginia might be going rogue anyway. And you're not leaving without me, daddy." Baer laughed.

Smithe almost laughed. Instead, he went on. "This Covid bull-crap is giving me the willies. I know it will take a couple of years to get it up and running like here."

"I know some guys, former Seals, Rangers, CIA, that are into building specialized housing. They call their company *Home Restorations*".

"Do you trust them? You know what I mean."

"With my life."

"Hook me up with them, okay?" Smithe looked up at a picture of George Washington on the wall.

"I will, but you have to go through me. They are extremely off the grid."

"Great, no problem. Get them ASAP."

"I'll get on it right away," Baer promised.

"You coming over today to be debriefed about Florida?" Smithe was anxious.

"I'll be over."

After the debriefing Smithe said, "I'm sending you to Oklahoma to look at the properties my people picked out."

"They found something already? What's the matter, you don't trust your people?"

"Of course I do," Smithe barked, "I want to see what you think. Your piece will be next to mine. See if you like it."

Baer looked at his folded hands, "I don't have a say?"

"Of course you do. But you know you. And you know I'll pick it right."

Defeated but not bitter, he knew John was right. "When?"

"Tomorrow. It's east of Heavener. Hilly and wooded. I think it will be perfect."

"If you like it, I'll like it." Baer hoped that would put an end to the discussion.

"Crap. We'll both go and take a look see. I want us to be sure."

"I still have that Gannon guy to get."

"Lucky for him, we'll do this first."

"Okay, by me. What about the client?"

"This is a business move. He's not privy to the workings of our organization. We haven't broken the contract. We keep our word."

"Good to hear," Baer said.

"You bet." Smithe rang for Jeeves.

John Smithe and Jake Baer drove to Dulles and hitched a ride on Mr. Harjo's corporate jet—a Gulfstream G650. Mr. Harjo, a former financial backer of Smithe, was the president of Oneida Oil Company, headquartered in OK.

As the jet roared down the runway, Baer held up his drink in a salute to Smithe and spoke. "One to go. Let's drink to his unhealth."

Smithe smiled, held up his glass. "To his demise." He drank.

Baer said, "Hear, hear." He drank it all in one gulp.

They landed at Wiley Post Airport, situated in Bethany, Oklahoma, a small town *inside* of north west Oklahoma City. They also borrowed Mr. Harjo's driver and black Ford SUV limo to get to Heavener, three and a half hours away, in LeFlore County in eastern Oklahoma. In Heavener the driver took Burn Lane E which became E1460 county road. They continued driving east to Runestone Park, that led to the Park entrance. They came upon the park entrance and went through the entrance and followed the road SE then NE. Shortly the road became dirt that led to the property and they continued to the site. Thanks to the for-sale signs they found it with no trouble. They could see the start of a couple of trails that ran throughout the property. A steal at $72,000 for each 80 acres, and very close to the Oklahoma, Arkansas State lines.

In the SUV Baer said, "That small town, Heaven-ner, is close by. I think that is a plus."

Smithe laughed. So did the driver.

Baer asked, "What?"

In between gulps of laughing, Smithe explained, "It's pronounced *heev ner.*"

"How was I suppose to know? I've never been in this part of Oklahoma."

"Smithe chuckled and said, "Thanks for the laugh."

After the driver parked, they all disembarked, stretched and waited for the realtor. Two minutes later he pulled up. Getting out of his pick up the realtor waved.

"Howdy, y'all." He walked over to them. "I'm, Tom Banks." They shook hands. "Got some papers to guide you." He handed them the papers. "Y'all take your time. The stakes mark the boundaries. Call me tonight or tomorrow and let me know what y'all think. Then we can visit." Smithe said okay and Banks left.

Baer said, "Isn't y'all singular and all y'all, plural?"

Smithe looked at him and shook his head. The driver chuckled. Then Smithe walked toward a stake. Baer yelled after him, "I'm trying to learn English here."

They checked out and walked the frontage of both 80 acres that were next to each other. They stayed close to the road. Baer then went a little farther in and came back.

"Looks good," said Baer.

The land lay south of Dry Creek, in reality a dry creek bed. The leaves on the trees made it hard to gauge the layout of the land. As they walked it more, they had a general idea and it suited them perfectly. They also discussed Jerry Gannon.

"It's going to be tricky getting close to the house so I'm thinking of some way to lure him out. Maybe that I've got a message from Turner. Got to meet him somewhere that's public and private," Baer said.

"A mall. Pick a mall," Smithe spat his gum out.

"Good idea." Baer looked around. "You know I like it here already. I think you picked a great spot for the Underground and house."

"I'm thinking of putting the house in the middle of the acreage with the Underground separate from the house this time."

"How come?"

"If the house ever gets raided, they won't find the nerve center. I'll hide it in plain sight."

"How're you going to do that, John." Baer looked at the trees, thick on all sides.

"Picture this," Smithe began, "it'll be under the trees—in the ground. The entrance will be a hollowed-out tree. One of the big round ones, if any." He gazed around but didn't see any big enough. "Or maybe under a large bush. Or we'll make a large faux tree."

"And ride an elevator down," Baer taunted.

"Not a bad idea, but no, a spiral staircase for going down."

Laughing Baer said, "What, the staircase doesn't go up?"

"That's a great idea. It will be collapsed so to speak with spikes or sharp razors. Pull a lever from below to make it stairs." *Hmmm.* Smithe played with his chin. Smithe mumbled, "No one would go down a slide with spikes and razors." *How to get down quick if the need arises? Could a fire pole be hidden?*

"I'll bite. How do you get down?"

"Fire pole in the middle."

Baer started to laugh then abruptly stopped. "That's not a bad idea."

"And a spiral staircase for going up or down."

"So, use the fire pole if one is in a hurry."

"Yes. Come on, lad. It's getting late. We'll discuss it on the drive back." Smithe looked around again. "Damn, it's good to be back in Oklahoma. Well son, what do you think?"

"Perfect. I say go for it," Baer urged.

Smithe called the realtor. "Well take it. Come here with the paperwork."

Fifteen minutes later the realtor drove up. He jumped out of his truck and laid some papers on the hood and placed magnets to hold them in place.

"You guys made up your minds quick. Read over everything before you sign," He said.

Smithe and Baer went over to glance through them.

"Nothing seems to be a miss here," Smithe said.

"Looks good to me," Baer concurred.

"Are you gentlemen sure?" the realtor squinted.

Smithe answered, "Yes. My bank will send your bank the funds."

"I'll need some earnest money with the signatures."

Smithe walked over to him and put his arm around him and patted his shoulder. "Sonny, you might not know me. I'm John Smithe, the former senator of this great state. My word is good." He let go.

The realtor looked at him a second then said, "Well I'll be danged. You are. I always voted for you. No hard feelings and no money." He stuck out his hand and they shook.

After that Smithe and Baer signed.

Heavener was over 41% Mexican, and most of them worked at the chicken plant. That didn't bother Baer or Smithe. Some might even be illegal. That was a state problem; and that would make the people mind their own business.

Baer called his man after the signing, to start planning to build. Both houses at once—and the Underground. The retired Ranger builder said he and four co-partners would be there tomorrow for a look/see and get started ASAP. He promised to be finished in four months, before the weather got too cold.

The former Ranger and his partners did contract some of the work out to other veterans in the building business. All of them were tight lipped.

The drive was long but it gave Baer more time to brainstorm with John Smithe. After discussing the new Underground, Baer got back to business.

"Let's scope out some malls close to Takoma Park," Baer said. "Let me borrow your iPad."

"Here. Have at it," Smithe said handing the instrument, as he called it, to Baer.

Baer searched and found a mall named Downtown Silver Spring. Scrolling and checking it out Baer said, "This looks good. Parking off of Wayne Avenue. Indoor/outdoor with tables and chairs to sit and talk or eat. I could bring him there and while we're still in the parking lot I'd invite him into my SUV."

"No, "Smithe said. "You get in his. Make sure you wear gloves, disguise…"

"John," Baer interrupted, "I know what to do. I talk out loud when I'm planning. Let me talk. No, I don't invite him in my car. I'll suggest his, where he'll feel safe—and I wouldn't have to drag his sorry ass back to his car."

"Good. Good," Smithe said.

"Small talk first, then the down and dirty."

"Excellent."

"He'll know exactly why he's being killed."

"Sounds easy breezy," Smithe admitted.

"Sounds can be deceiving," Baer warned.

They discussed more strategies all the way to Wiley Post Airport.

On the flight back, Baer and Smithe had talked with the geeks, by iPhone, to set things up with the builders. They used their own code because they didn't trust any modern electronic device.

The Gulfstream G650 landed at Dulles in the dark but they still had time for dinner at Smithe's house. While eating at Smithe's house, Baer got a call on his cell from Home Restorations as an unknown number. Baer answered it knowing it was them. Very few people knew his number and only theirs came up as unknown.

"Baer."

"Jake, it's Rob O'Rielly. We can start Monday. Your guys are sending us the coordinates and Meriwether said he would be there to meet us with plans, ASAP." Lewis had used the Meriwether alias as he did with everyone outside of the "family".

"As you know, lion fart, "Baer began, "cost won't be an issue, but we want top quality."

"Hey dog breath, you know that's what we do."

"Letting you know, dip-shit, that I won't have time to visit the site until I finish the job I have. So you'll be in good hands with Meriwether."

"Great. Is there a way we can come in from the opposite direction? From Arkansas?"

"Hell, I don't know, you dumb son of a bitch. Look at a map."

"Roger. Talk to you later, fake SEAL fly crap."

"Be looking forward to it. Have a good day, numb nuts."

After Baer hung up, Smithe looked at him worried. "Were you two calling each other foul names?"

Smiling Baer said, "Yeah. That's what Navy Seals do. Sometimes it rubs off onto the Rangers. I'm always honored that I'm included in their verbiage."

Smithe thought he saw a tear in his eye. "Gee, such a bunch of ruffians." Smithe spit out his gum into an ashtray.

"We usually do better than that but my using low-key insults, he knew I wasn't alone. He knows lion fart means that I'm with someone."

"Damn, you guys are tough."

"You bet."

"Well, tough guy, we need to talk about your lady friend."

"When I finish the job. Okay?"

"For now." Smithe had other ideas. He'd do it on the sly.

23

Gerald George Gannon grew tired of listening to the phone ring and no one answered. He disconnected. Something strange was going on. Especially since Scott would know it was Gannon calling.

Talking to himself, since Gloria left him forever, the bitch. "It ain't like Scott not answering his phone. He always jumps on it. Damn, something musta happened. Probably dead, like the rest. Shit!"

Scared, he paced around his small living room—thinking—out loud. "I think I have his dumb-ass wife's number someplace."

His hands shaking a bit, he took a small black phonebook out of the lamp table's drawer. He kept certain people in the book, not in his phone. More private. He turned the pages until he got to the Ts. Running his finger down the list, he stopped. He dialed her number on his iPhone. He was about to hang up when a strange female voice answered.

"Oh, I'm sorry. I musta dialed wrong. I was calling a Claudia."

"This is her phone. Who's this?"

"A friend of her husband. I can't reach him on his phone. Sorry."

"Wait. What is your name?"

"Who wants to know?" he asked roughly.

"The Charlotte County Sheriff, deputy Leif. Now, WHO are you?"

"I'm a friend of Scott Turner. Where is he?"

"We don't know. Would you mind coming to the sheriff's office for an interview." Not a question.

"Hell no. In Florida? I'm calling from Maryland." *Whoops and damn.* He continued anyway. "What's happened to him? Where is he and why did you answer his wife's phone?"

"Evidently you don't know. He's missing."

"Missing. Like how? When?"

"Three days ago, Mister…"

Gannon thought quickly. His name truthfully or fake?

"Erving. Boris Erving. Where's Claudia?"

"Mr. Erving, Claudia's in the hospital for a heart attack. How do you know the Turners?"

"I've done some business with him a couple of months ago. Why do you think he's missing?"

"I should be asking the questions, Mister Erving. What kind of business?"

At first Gannon was pissed, now he was confused. "Uh, just business, private."

"Mister Erving, this is serious. If you know where he is…"

"I don't know!" he yelled. "That's why I called his wife and got you instead! He was supposed to call me two days ago. He didn't. So now I called him and got you! What happened?" he shouted.

"Calm down, sir. You seem mighty interested for being a casual business partner. I'll tell you this, we're not sure. He left the house Sunday with an acquaintance and never came home. His wife was in hysterics and had a heart attack. Got the call, and here we are with you. We're having the FBI come in on this. Now it's your turn to answer some questions."

Gannon was shocked. He couldn't say anything but he heard in a low voice deputy Leif saying to someone, thanks.

"Thanks for what?" Gannon asked, his tone normal now.

"We ran your number Mister Gannon. Would you like to tell me something or would you like the FBI at your door?"

"Send the jerks. I won't be around. I didn't do it. Somebody's after us. I'm the last one, and I'm outta here. Let the FBI find HIM. Isn't that what they do? Find Bodies Instantly?" He hung up.

Gannon couldn't believe it. Somebody was killing them all. He gave the cops that phony name now they think they have a reason to harass him. Shit.

He ran upstairs, grabbed two large suitcases and started packing. He would leave his phone here and buy a burner. He threw his revolver, a Smith&Wesson Model 67, 4" barrel, into one of the suitcases and a full box of self-defense .38 special. Dumped some clothes on top, then filled the other suitcase with more clothes.

He didn't know where to go but he wasn't staying home. He hurried out to his car and tossed the suitcases into the trunk. Back up the stairs into the house he grabbed his checkbook, bank cards, and some cash. He locked the house and hurried down the stairs to his car. Jumped in and quickly, but not too fast, drove up the street and made a right on Tenth Avenue, that led him to East-West Highway.

Having been a stevedore made him physically tough. Mentally he couldn't think calmly. Panic had kicked cockiness out of the way. Calming himself down he drove to the bank and closed his bank and charge account. He left with cash.

After he calmed down some more, he could think. Now he knew where to go. To his brother's place in West Virginia.

The day after Smithe and Baer got back from Oklahoma, Baer drove buy Gannon's house slowly. He had to. Prince Georges County police cars were scattered along the street and some on the sidewalk. He noticed the FBI cars were there also. *Damn, what the hell happened?* He'd have to find out from Clark and Lewis. He called Smithe.

"Somethings happened. Pee Gee County cops and FBI are all over Gannon's house. See if the guys can find out why," Baer said.

"Will do. I'll call you back. Where're staying?"

"Some dump in Silver Spring."

"Do you have the scrambler?"

"Of course."

"I'll call you on that." Smithe hung up. Then he called the Underground. Lewis answered.

"What's up, doc?"

"Okay, Bugs, you and Clark get with Quark and find out what's happening at Jerry Gannon's house."

"We're on it." Lewis disconnected.

Baer headed back to his motel as quickly as he could, without stirring up any cops. In his room he grabbed his suitcase and threw it on the bed. The scrambler rang. Baer answered, "Tell me."

Smithe gave him the whole story including all the bad news. "He's in the wind. TSA is checking all flights out of the country. They even have Interpol on it, checking flights coming from the U.S., looking at airport cameras. The guys are feeding Quark with a ton of info to go through. Hopefully we'll have an answer within an hour. Turner's wife had a heart attack and Quark found out that Gannon called while the Sheriff was at Turner's house. That got the Sheriff's department moving. They think Gannon killed him and stashed him."

Baer hadn't expected that. He also wasn't going to second guess their fuzzy thinking. "That's good. But I don't think even Quark will find him, John. I don't think he left the country."

"Why not?"

"Because he knows he's not smart enough to cross the border."

"He might surprise you."

"Probably, but I doubt it."

"Suppose he goes to Alaska?"

"Not likely, John. He'll stick close to Maryland. Maybe cross over to Virginia or West Virginia. I'm trying to remember something."

"He has enough money to go farther."

Baer was silent for a moment, his mind wandered. Maybe he would be stupid enough take a plane. His mind shifted to Jane and her being a stewardess for an airline. He wondered how she was doing and what she was doing.

Smithe asked, "Are you there? Well, do you think he's in a faraway state?"

Baer's mind quickly shifted back to the problem. "I'm still thinking."

With Jane off his mind, he remembered what Turner said after he had stopped the tape. "Turner said, and this was not recorded, that Gannon had a cousin living in eastern West Virginia. The cousin has a small cabin. Have Quark look up all Gannons in West Virginia. I'll wait."

"Hold on."

While he was on hold, Baer started packing. Less than four minutes later, "Jake, you there?"

"What do you have?"

"There are five Gannon's in West Virginia."

"Read me the names and the cities."

Smithe started reading the first names and the cities. Smithe came to the third location and name.

"Stop. That's it, Timothy Gannon in Frost."

"How do you know?"

"I'd bet Tim is his cousin and he went there. Frost is in the eastern part of the state. Get Quark to give me details. I'm going to need the drones.

That's rough and hidden country there. Backwoods—hillbilly heaven. You couldn't find a skunk there even if he sprayed."

"What's your next move?"

"I'm coming home—packing my stuff for a trip to Frost."

24

Gannon was scared shitless and ditched his car on a side street in Silver Spring. He walked to an Enterprise rental close by. He had a false I.D. with a false driver's license and insurance just in case a day like this came, and it came fast. Gannon used it at the car rental. Picked out a car then drove to D.C. Beltway I-495, then to I-66W, to hook up with I-81S. Later, he connected with WV-92 heading south to the town of Frost in Pocahontas County, West Virginia. He drove through Frost, a town so small it was only around one mile long, east to west, and a quarter of a mile north to south. He passed the fire department, passed the Methodist church and right away passed Dean's Den Takeout, it took 30, maybe 40-45 seconds to go through Frost. Jerry Gannon hoped he'd locate his cousin's house from his foggy memory. It was about 2 miles west from Frost.

He kept doing the speed limit until he approached Wildcat Hollow, near where the ghost town of Sunset used to be. He slowed a bit looking for a specific driveway on the left. He spotted it and took the driveway to a house and passed the house. To an outsider it looked like it dead ended at the house, but a rugged trail continued upward towards the woods and beyond. His cousin had told him to follow that path to his house. The rental he drove took a beating on the rocky, hilly, twisting road with tree roots and branches beating at the car. He crossed over Knapp Creek, to where his cousin's cabin sat. He figured two miles more but it seemed longer. It was hard to judge—he didn't look at the odometer, he just followed the path. Tim Gannon lived close to the Virginia State line and told his cousin some years back that he could spit into Virginia. Tim had a habit of telling tall tales.

Gannon continued the climb slowly; he didn't want the rental to break down where it would tie his cousin or himself to any crimes.

Tim's cabin sat up in the hills between Frost and the ghost town of Sunset, but closer to Sunset. To the east, across the state line in Virginia, the town of Sunrise was alive.

Jerry Gannon pulled up cautiously to the cabin. *Crap. This is gonna be rough staying here. But better than being dead.* He'd put up with it until things cooled down.

Gradually Gannon slid out of his car. He didn't want to spook Tim. Tim had no electricity, no phone. Just oil lamps and a fireplace and bottled water.

"Hey, cousin Tim! It's me! Cousin Jerry from Maryland," he yelled.

Immediately, a voice. "Come to the door and no tricks."

"I'm not funning you Tim. It's Jerry come to see you." Jerry stepped up to the door. "It's okay to open the door. I'm alone."

Jerry heard a deadbolt slide near the bottom of the door, then a turn of another deadbolt at head level. Tim had made it to swing both ways, in or out. Tim slowly pulled the door open inward. Jerry saw two large gaping holes of an eight-gauge double barrel shotgun aimed at his stomach. He jumped back.

"For crap sake Tim put that gun down."

Tim's eyes showed in the crack. "Is that really you, Jerry?"

"Yes it's me."

The door swung open and Tim stood with a smile and his arms wide open, with the 8 gauge still in his right hand. Jerry walked up to him and they hugged.

"Good to see you, cousin Jerry."

"Good to see you, Tim. You can put that cannon away now."

"Sure, sure. Come on in and we'll have some corn."

"You still making that corn liquor?"

"Does a bear shit in the woods?"

"Well bring it on, cause I'm in trouble and need your help."

"No problem, cousin. Sit. I'll get the jug. You don't need a glass, do you?"

"Nope."

"Good. Cause you ain't a gittin' one. We'll drink like real men."

The two sat at a small handmade wood table across from each other passing the jug. Jerry told a short cut version of his side of the story as Tim rested the large jug on his shoulder and took a swig.

Jerry finished by saying, "So somehow the law thinks my friend's in trouble and they want to tie me in."

Tim scratched his facial stubble, thinking.

Jerry squinted his eyes looking past Tim to the back of the cabin. He blinked. "Are those trees I see or is that realistic wallpaper."

"Shit, Jerry, that ain't no wallpaper."

Jerry's jaw dropped, "You mean that's open to the outside."

"Of course. Keeps it cool in the summer and in the winter the wind don't blow this way. Naked trees stops it anyways. And a nice fire makes it warm. Ran out of wood to finish the back. Trees growed right up to make a wall—kinda."

"Gosh damn, Tim, don't critters get in?"

"Nope. Got traps set. Bear traps, small critter traps. All kinds of traps out yonder. So don't go out without me. And sometimes I even catch dinner." Tim laughed like he told the funniest joke ever.

"Man, you're tough. What about people?"

"I don't bother them and they don't bother me. Like I said, don't go wandering without me. Besides my traps, there're briers and stickers and thorn bushes all over. Hear 'em coming a mile away," he said smiling. "No law dogs'll sneak on us. Still it won't be easy to spot them, if they get sneaky. Notice muh door? Swings both ways. Cool, huh?"

"How cold does it get here in the fall and winter?"

"We get a lot of frost mostly. That's why the town's called Frost. Clever, ain't it?"

"Sounds cold to me."

"What are you, a pussy?"

Jerry grabbed the jug. "Never mind. I got my .38 Special with me and ammo," Jerry told him.

"Good. That and my eight gauge will leave 'em hurtin."

Jerry said, "Tomorrow you and me will ditch this rental in Virginia, maybe thirty miles away. That should be good." He continued looking around the place with its weird designed curtains. He squinted to see better. They weren't designs, that was dirt, and webs, and other things he couldn't identify.

"Works for me," Tim said.

"What do you drive?"

"An eighty-nine, F-150."

"Guess I'll have to get me a truck."

"Be best." Tim yawned. "Best get some sleep now."

"How about we eat?"

"Help yourself to that loaf of bread. You sleep on the cot, since you are company. I got the floor mattress." With that he blew out the lamp.

"What about my bread?"

"Get it. It's by the sink. Early to bed. Early to rise. Good night, Jerry."

Jerry thought, what the hell, and felt his way to the cot. He found it and laid on his back. *How'd the hell did I get into this mess? Someone spilled their guts.*

In the morning after they ate whatever it was, Jerry wouldn't even try to guess, and after they finished cleaning the plates, they headed out the front door.

Jerry asked, "Do you get mail here?"

"Heck, no. I don't want the damn feds to know I even exist."

"Sounds good to me, Tim."

"Follow me and don't talk to nobody. I'll do the talking. We'll dump that car where they won't find it for years."

That really sounded good to Jerry.

They traveled east into Virginia and around eighty to ninety miles later they entered the north entrance to Blue Ridge Parkway. They drove south until Tim pulled over and got out of his truck. He walked up to Jerry and said, "Up ahead is a big drop with a flimsy wood fence. We'll make sure no one's coming and I'll drive the car through the fence, jump out, and down she goes. Where she'll stop no one will find it for a good long while."

"Let's do it," Jerry said.

What they actually did, after thinking about it, was put the car in neutral, cut the engine, then both pushed it through the flimsy wood fence. It smashed through the fence with ease and made a racket going down—but no explosion.

Once back at the cabin, Jerry felt better. He had to start making plans to hide elsewhere but going there will have to wait until things blew over. He had Tim drive him over to Marlinton so he could buy an AM & FM battery radio. He needed to keep tabs on the world. The closest town with a Wal Mart was over 2 ½ hours away. They had nothing better to do, so they went there also.

Back at the cabin they listened to the radio, but nothing about Gannon aired. They sat at the table eating boiled pigs' feet and drinking corn whiskey from the jug.

Tim said, "What you did was a long time ago. What the law do, just wake up?"

"No. I think someone squealed. I'd like to kill 'em, but someone else did."

"Good," said Tim. "You know cuz, I've been thinking, if you think someone's coming after you, I have a couple of good ol' boys that would love some action."

"Well, I don't know if anyone will come. I hope they never find me."

"I'm gonna jump in the truck and bring them here for a few nights. Just on the safe side. Ain't it."

"You still got the Baltimore, Polish lingo with you."

"Old habits hard to break." Tim got up. "I'll get them now. Hold down the fort."

"Wait," Jerry said. "Look for a good used truck for me, also."

"We'll do that in a coupla days, fer sure." Tim left happy.

An hour later Tim returned with what looked like two cast members from the movie, *Deliverance*, but they bore no resemblance to Burt Reynolds. They got out of the truck and went inside, through the front door. Tim told them to put their Remington 770, 30.06's in the corner and their ammo. Tim introduced one as Big John and the other as Little Pete. Big John's hair looked like a short version of Ben Franklin's.

"Big John here moves slow but shoots fast. Right?" Tim asked.

"You bet," Big John answered smiling with two missing top front teeth.

"Little Pete moves fast and shoots faster," Tim said.

Little Pete grinned and had three bottom teeth missing. He lifted a skinny arm to scratch his unruly mop of black hair.

"Yeah, but he can't hit nuttin'," Big John said.

"The hell I can't. I can out shoot you any day of the week."

Tim said, "Now boys—cut it out."

Big John grabbed Little Pete around the neck and pulled his head to him. Then with a knuckled fist, rubbed the top of his head. "I was just funning with Lil' Pete."

"Let me go, John. Dang." Pete pulled away and held the top of his head.

Jerry thought, *oh brother. I hope they are worth the trouble.*

"Come on over here youze guys and grab the jug." Tim sat and took a swig and passed it around. Each one took a slug. Tim had plenty of corn liquor stashed away to last for weeks.

Tim said, "My cuz here has some problems with the feds."

"And the Maryland and Florida police. They think I killed a friend of mine, which I didn't. I've never been to Florida in my life. I ran here because someone else killed my friend." He looked at the locals. "And I know he's after me—to kill me!"

"Why?" said Big John reaching for the jug.

"Me and the one that got killed was in a group in high school and we got into some trouble over a girl."

"That'll do it," said Lil' Pete, reaching for the jug.

"Well, someone broke our pact and now some clown is killing all of us." He grabbed the jug, took a swig and yelled, "I'm the last one!"

"The last one what?" Lil' Pete asked.

"The last one of the group that ain't killed." Jerry thought what a moron. What was Tim thinking?

Tim broke in, "That's whys youze guys are here. In case the clown comes here."

"He knows Jerry's here?" Big John asked.

"I don't know that for sure but the killer is finding everyone else and pops them," Jerry said.

"So we're here to protect Jerry and make sure the killer don't leave here on his own." Tim said. He took a swig and passed it to Jerry.

"He won't get you, Jerry, as long as I'm around," Big John said.

"And he's around and around and way around." Lil' Pete laughed.

"Shut your skinny face, boy."

Lil' Pete just laughed.

Tim said, "Here's what we're gonna do. When we go to get supplies youze guys stay here and keep your eyes and ears open. I got plenty of animal traps out yonder so youze can hear anybody coming. If you see or hear anything, shoot first. Then see what you got."

They said, okay and kept drinking. They also spent the night. Jerry didn't feel any safer. They could start a ruckus and get the local law here. He had a fitful sleep.

25

"That's great news," Karl Kephart said to Lance Pruitt on his iPhone. Kephart informed Pruitt that he was on speaker.

Pruitt had just informed him that another one bit the dust. Karl was in his Ford 350 truck checking part of his herd.

The ranchers were continuing raising more beef because of what he thought was a phony pandemic. Karl was one rancher to be doing a booming business. He knew the virus was real but the hysteria surrounding it was hype. Some of the ranchers and farmers were doing well because of it. Others were not because of closed or cut backs in the restaurant sector. He knew the grocery stores were picking up business, taking up the slack from the restaurants. That would help now, but what about the future?

He saw the cotton, wheat, sunflowers for the seeds, alfalfa, hay, you name it and Oklahoma was producing. Also, oil was still booming. He knew that the Dry Creek city area, south of El Reno, where Lance Pruitt lived, that oil rigs were going up then taken down to be moved to a new location. The "old" locations were "capped" for storage or pumping. Pipelines were still being buried. Since all of this was on private lands, some ranchers and private citizens were getting extra money for the oil pumped and/or the buried pipelines. The companies that worked on federal lands or had federal contracts were screwed.

Kephart hoped his good times would continue.

"Yes, it is. Only one more to go," Pruitt confirmed.

"Money well spent—I'd say."

"Well, speaking of money, they'll need more for the last one." Lance heard Karl breathe deeply into the phone.

Kephart had stopped driving. "And why is that? They're not trying to milk me. Are they? I don't like to be yanked around." Karl really didn't like to spend more than he had to. He was tough but realistic.

"No, nothing like that. The last one, Jesse Gannon, disappeared and hasn't been found yet."

"Disappeared? What the…damn it, Lance."

"He'll get found but to do that it's going to cost. They think he's out of state. Not in Maryland anymore."

"How the hell did that happen? Never mind. How much?"

"The go between said he wasn't sure but let's start with two thousand dollars."

"Would they accept an ounce and a quarter of gold?"

Lance thought quickly before he answered for the paladins. "They would but not at this time. They need cash for the operation. I have no doubt they will accept gold for a final payment."

"Okay. But they want gold for the final payment, correct?"

Pruitt felt cornered. "I think that was my understanding."

"Don't matter. Just get the bastard. Makes me feel good the others are in Hell."

When Karl came home, Betty asked, "How's the herd doing?"

"Great. We're making a killing on this stupid pandemic. The bulls are busy keeping the herd growing."

"My stomach hurts. I'm going to lie down." Betty held her stomach.

"Covid nerves again?"

"Yes."

"Even though business is booming I wish they'd quit this crap. Don't worry about that disease. I heard Sars was worse and no one did crap about it. At the same time the seasonal flu was in full bloom. Not to mention Tuberculosis, which killed one point five million people in twenty-nineteen. I don't trust the so-called authorities. I think the COVID-19 numbers are skewed. So, honey, please don't worry about it. It's to control us."

"Yeah." He didn't convince her and she made her way to the bedroom. Her nerves were getting to her again.

Poor woman. Damn politicians, raping the people; Karl thought.

Their Homeopathic doctor had them take a formulation of colostrum to boost their immune system. He also told them not to get the flu shots. Loaded with crap; monkey virus, and the corona virus, plus other unsavory ingredients, he told them. Neither one had been sick for years. Now, on top of everything else, his wife was making herself sick because of politics.

Baer was at his house packing like he was going camping—one never knew in this business. He planned on driving the SUV to West Virginia. Lots of rough roads and hills, not to mention back trails and forest areas. For that he took a couple of the small drones, cameras only. He felt that this was not going to be easy. Well, that's why he gets paid the big bucks.

He called Smithe. "Any new details?"

"Yes, Enterprise in Silver Spring, on Georgia Avenue, reported that one of their rentals is missing. Not back on time. Can't reach the person. Probably a fake I.D. and phone number."

"How'd he pay?"

"Stolen or fake charge card."

"Of course. Any cameras in the store?"

"No. If he's smart, he won't be using that fake ID anymore."

"Going to be work locating him but I have a general idea where he is, thanks to Quark and the guys."

"And also, Turner. He told you West Virginia."

"Yeah, can't forget that jerk. Well, I'm leaving now fer West Virginie."

"Be careful, my boy."

"I will. I won't be taking 'Killer Looking', just the camera drones. Killer will be too noisy over there. No place to blend. I'll have to make it a quiet job also."

"It's your call."

It was almost mid-day when Baer arrived in Frost, Pocahontas County. He stuck out. He'd have to think how he would do this. Got to find a motel, but it won't be in Frost. He found one in Marlinton, in The Seneca State Park. He called Smithe on the scrambler letting him know of his arrival.

"By the way," Smithe said, "The FBI found Gannon's abandoned car in Silver Spring."

"Let me guess, the car rental is in walking distance."

"Yes. FBI had the Montgomery County LEOs combed every street within a mile and found his car a quarter of a mile away. So, they found it quickly."

"Good for them. Doesn't help us any. I'm setting up in the Old Clark Inn, in Marlinton for the night. It's a quaint old B and B here." He gave Smithe the room number.

"Good night, son. And be careful."

"Again?" Baer laughed.

"Just be careful." The older Smithe got, the closer he felt towards Jake.

In the morning Baer left the Old Clark Inn and drove about 10 miles to WV 92 at Minnehaha Springs and took 92 back towards Frost. The cut-in driveway would be on his right. He found it and immediately there was a snag.

He said aloud to no one, "There's no place to be inconspicuous. You'd think in West Virginia there would be beaucoup hiding spaces."

He couldn't even get food at Dean's Den Takeout because he would be remembered, so he brought his lunch. Baer needed to get the small drone in the air. He'd look out of place anywhere he parked. The chances were high that someone would come up to him and ask if he needed help. Then he thought of something—he'd eat his lunch now.

He spotted two areas that looked good and picked one with few trees and next to a large open field. He had pointed the SUV facing south, south-west, which was the way out of town. After he parked, he spread his lunch out on the hood of his SUV, then he got the drone ready. Out of the car, he set it down, grabbed the control box and let it take off towards the approximate coordinates the geeks had sent. This would be tricky, keeping one eye on the drone screen and the other on anyone coming. He took a folding chair out of the car and set it next to the vehicle up front on the side not facing the road. He laid the drone controls and screen on the chair while he took a few bites of his lunch. A pick-up truck drove by and Baer waved at the same time the pick-up driver waved. His lunch on the hood worked. After he finished his lunch, he opened the passenger door and moved the chair, with the drone equipment, there to hide it better. He left the remnants of lunch on the hood and went back to the chair and sent the drone on its way.

The drone sent very clear pictures back as it flew over the trees toward the suspected site. Noticing the problem quickly, he mumbled *crap*. There were very few open spaces between the trees. The closer he flew to the cabin the thicker the trees. To try to get close and look through the leaves was a tricky maneuver. Finally reaching the cabin he saw that the trees were right up against the back of the house. Looked like no way in from the back. Moving to the front there was more open space and he saw an old Ford pick-up.

He brought the drone down a little and didn't see any other vehicles. They could be out…or, Jerry Gannon wasn't there. He chanced bringing the drone down a little more on the side of the shack. Looked like a shack to him. One small window on this side. Next, he flew over to the other side. Another small window. He didn't want to chance a drop down in the front, but somehow he'd have to get a look. He flew to the front again. The mic picked up some voices he couldn't make out. It was more than one person though. Now it sounded like just two. He took a chance and pointed the drone camera towards the front.

"Great! That's Jerry." Baer smiled. Jerry was standing out front with Tim in the doorway.

What came next wasn't great.

"What the hell is that? Damndest bird I ever seen." Tim cried.

Jerry swung his head around. "That ain't no bird! That's a drone. Get your shotgun!"

"What?"

"Get your damn gun and shoot it."

Tim ran into the house. Baer had seen and heard enough and zipped the drone high and fast. Then he flew it south, taking a roundabout route to return it. He landed it and put it into the back seat. He'd stow it later. He dismantled his mess on the hood and got back on the road and drove in a southerly direction taking a long roundabout way to get back to Marlinton.

Tim came rushing out. "Where's that thing!?" Pointing his scattergun up. "Gone now! Shit. Who in the hell is that? Jerry, you got revenuers after you?"

Also, Big John and Lil Pete came out quickly. "Revenuers?" Big John asked.

"Hell no. Nobody knows what I do here and it ain't none of their beeswax."

Tim was older and had gone to school in Dundalk but tried to sound like a hillbilly, except when he got riled up.

Angrier now than a nest full of disturbed hornets he shouted, "So, you're here because YOU'RE in big trouble. Ain't it. YOU did killed your friend."

"No. Really, cuz."

"Don't cuz me. Damn, you brought the Feds with you."

"No, nothing like that. Let's go inside and I'll tell you the whole story."

"You damn site you will. But I'm scouting first to make sure there's no others around. You go inside."

"There won't be any more drones."

"I'm scouting humans. Get inside."

Jerry did as told. So did the other two.

An hour later Tim came back. "Tell me," he said as he put the shotgun on the wall hanger. "All of it. I can't believe this is just over a girl."

The *Deliverance* guys were all ears.

"I'm going to stock up on food, water, ammo and supplies in Marlinton at the Appalachian Sport store in town. You stay here and keep inside with your head down," Tim told his cousin. "I don't want nobody to know you're here. Or you two either."

"Somebody already does," Jerry replied downhearted. He had a feeling all of this was connected to the rape five decades ago. He had gotten away with all of the later rapes, he thought. So, it had to be that one from the party. Damn, times have changed. Who the hell was after him and how did he find him?

"I'm talking about the locals, you dope."

"I know. I think this guy killed all the others. I checked it out. I'm the last one in that group. This ain't random. I'm the last, Tim!"

"Don't get your bowels in an uproar. We'll get this clown. You and me, Cousin. Family together." He walked towards the door. "Be back soon."

Big John said, "We're behind you too."

"And in front if need be," Lil' Pete said.

Tim came back after fifty-two minutes. Jerry kept watching the clock the whole time he was gone. Nothing else to do.

"Help me get this stuff inside," Tim said.

"Man, you musta bought out the store."

"Pert near," Tim said smiling. "This could be fun."

The four men busied themselves for an hour setting things up, making gun slots in the windows, stacking ammo at the front door and in back, next to the trees. Also, the side windows.

"Here, I borrowed this twelve gauge for you. It's a Mossberg Persuader, six shots before reloading. Got plenty of shells and two boxes of thirty-eights for your revolver. All I need is my eight gauge with plenty of double aughts."

They put food and water at each site.

"We will have to watch the windows. They could throw something in. If they do, throw it back out." They all nodded their heads.

Sweat poured down Jerry's face, armpits and back. Work and nerves.

"I ain't been in no firefight," Jerry pointed out. He loaded the shotgun with six shells. Finished, he wiped his forehead with his sleeve.

"Me neither," Tim finally said.

"We have," Lil' Pete remarked.

Big John slapped him upside of the head. "Shut up."

"What'll we do with the bodies?" Jerry asked.

"That's what I like to hear—positive thinking. Don't worry. I've got a good spot."

Big John and Lil' Pete cleaned and loaded their thirty aught sixes. They each had four, four round magazines and figured thirty-two shots total would be plenty. The rifles were bolt-action and they thought the rifles would be fast enough for their adversary, whoever it was. They had scopes on their rifles that wouldn't help them a bit in a shootout. They had no idea who they were up against. It wouldn't be a deer but a Baer.

26

At the Old Clark Inn, in his room, Baer called Robert Rocke on the scrambler.

"Hey, double R, you busy?"

"Not at the moment. What's up, Jake."

"I have one more wet work to do but I'll need you again for this one. He's hidden in a deep hole."

"For real or is that a metaphor?"

"For real. He's in some Podunk town in hillbilly heaven."

"You need me for that?" Rocke started laughing.

"Laugh all you want. This'll be like Nam."

"I'm not that old."

"You know what I mean. This guy is deep in the woods with his trigger-happy cousin, thinking I won't find him. Well, I found him at the same time he saw my drone."

"So? What's the problem? Blast him with the drone."

"I would, if I had Killer Looking. The situation is, I need to keep this off the radar like the others. You know how it is in our business."

"Yeh, I gotcha. What'll you need?"

"I need to get him from the front and the back of the cabin he's in. He's not alone. He has his cousin helping, which is no big deal but the layout calls for a two-prong attack. Front and back."

"You want me front or back?"

"Don't know yet but I'll take the toughest spot. I don't care if both are killed but I definitely want a guy named Jerry, killed." He didn't know there were four of them now.

"Might as well waste the other. Dead men tell no tales."

"That's debatable, but get here to, Marlinton, West Virginia, ASAP."

"Roger that. Give me the coordinates."

Rocke drove the 14 hours, all the way from Florida in his 2018 matte black Ford Expedition, filled with all the accoutrements for a small war. He still had plenty of room for a couple more guys. He was never one to bring too little to a fight. Always brought too much—one never knew. He stayed a little over the speed limits and only stopped for gas. He ate and drank as he drove.

When Rocke reached Marlinton, Baer was outside sitting on the porch. They went to Baer's room and waited until they were inside before they gave each other a hug and back slaps. Didn't want anyone to remember anything. The less motion, the less noticed.

"I brought flash bangs in case we need them." They were M84 stun grenades.

"Might need them but I don't want to use any. We're going to make too much noise as it is. I can have Killer Looking sent here. It's eight feet long and lots of firepower. It'll do the job but like I said, too much noise and fire. I want to do this as quick and quiet as possible," Baer reiterated.

"Q and Q. Understood. Going in with AR16s and nine mills, then?"

"I think that would be the best. With hush puppies." Meaning silencers or as they are formally known—sound suppressors.

"I take it you're not negotiating."

"No. Q and Q."

"Roger."

Baer smiled. "Good to see you, brotherman."

Rocke smiled back. "When do we start?"

"Tomorrow morning at oh one hundred hours. Let's get some sleep."

When they rose at midnight, a thunder storm raged. The lightning could be a problem. They wanted total darkness not flashes of light. The thunder— an asset. They grabbed something to eat and drink. They also packed food and water into two knapsacks. Each put on a belt that held four, nine-millimeter magazines for their Smith & Wesson 915 and another belt that held four magazines for the ARs. Each man had a total of 152 rounds of nine mm, and 302 rounds of 5.56mm NATO for the ARs. They made sure each weapon had one in the pipe. Overkill? No, again just prepared.

They loaded the magazines with latex gloves on. When they finished loading, they took the gloves off and set them aside. No fingerprints on the empty shell cases when they flew all over the place. The police were sure to comb the "battlefield".

When they dressed Rocke gave Baer a lightweight body armor that protected the chest and back. Rocke wore one too. "You never know," Rocke said.

"Yeah, don't take any chances, especially with Hillbillies," Baer said.

They left in Rocke's Expedition. They had flipped a coin before they left and Baer was to take the back of the shack. Rocke took the front.

Finding a spot to hide the Ford took a little time in the rain. When they found a good spot, Rocke drove straight into the woods until he couldn't go any farther. They got out and chopped some branches to hide the vehicle as best they could. They covered the taillights well. Flashes of lightning helped them a little with covering the SUV. They slung the ARs on their shoulders and rechecked their 9 mm. Smith & Wesson 915s on their right hips.

Putting on his night visons, Baer said, "It's about a mile that way according to this gizmo I got from Smithe."

The rain had let up and the lightning was now sporadic.

The "gizmo" was a Surface Planetary Coordinate Locator or SPCL, pronounced—Special. It picked up its information from Lewis and Clark's Underground via satellite.

The night was pitch dark, and the clouds seemed to make it darker. Baer followed the direction on the small screen keeping the arrow pointed toward the D at the top. Even with night vision goggles the going was slow and sometimes treacherous. Rocke slipped once on the rain-soaked ground and almost twisted his ankle. They carefully pushed away branches and ducked under some of the smaller trees. Sticker bushes and briar plants snagged at them often. Their weapons were wet but that didn't make any difference, unless one of them lost their grip because of the rain, which now had stopped.

Baer stopped and whispered, "We're one hundred yards from the front of the cabin. Turn on your mic." Baer moved away a couple of feet and whispered, "Do you copy?"

"Good and clear."

"Wait here until I maneuver around to the back. Then I'll tell you to move to fifty feet in front of the door. With all this foliage the concealment is good."

"Look, shit for brains, it's night and dark."

"Roger. Hey, dog breath, quit calling me names. I wasn't in the SEALs."

"Okay, man. That talk is only reserved for SEALs. But you're an honorary SEAL. Just make sure you have cover," commanded Rocke.

"Roger."

Baer moved away slowly trying not to snap any twigs. He got tangled again a couple of times in the sticker bushes. Then he ran into a damn bush with large stickie balls that clung to his vest and pants. His mind drifted off and Jane Stafford popped up. *When I finish here, I think I'll take her to Harbor Place.* A popular attraction in Baltimore. He approached the seventy-foot mark and stepped on something.

Snap!

He let a little yelp slip out. Rocke heard both the snap and the yelp.

"Jake, what happened?" he whispered into the mouthpiece.

"Stepped on a damn animal trap. Went through my boot. I'm trying to get the jaws open. Damn I need some kind of tool. Ouch! Damn that hurts."

"Traps can hurt," Rocke agreed.

"No, I stuck my hand on a couple of large sticker balls."

"Can you move forward?"

"No. I can't go anywhere. Remember? I'm trapped. Can't get it off. I'll have to make my stand here. Shit!"

"Copy. When I take the front, just start firing three bursts."

"Roger."

Earlier.

"Well good night, guys. I've got the back. You got the door. John, Pete, guard the sides but if we need help, jump right in."

"We're on point," Big John said.

"I'll be sleeping on my back, holding my gun on my chest," replied Jerry.

It was almost ten o'clock.

Around 1:30, Tim bolted upright. He had slept through the storm but now all was quiet. He thought he heard a slight yelp.

"Jerry!" Tim yelled quietly. "John!"

Jerry moaned softly.

"Get yer asses up! I heard somethink."

"Wha?" Jerry rubbed his eye.

John and Pete were wide awake and grabbed their 30-06 rifles.

Tim grabbed a 3,000 lumens tactical spotlight and shined it outside. He moved it side to side. He saw something that didn't look natural. "You out there! Get your damn hands in the air."

Baer had moved slow and silent, and now he stood. Even with his foot in the damn trap, his mind worked and pictured where they would be. From the outside it looked like a one room cabin with maybe a toilet and tub behind a wall.

A bright light suddenly hit him in the eyes and blinded his night vision goggles. He dropped. Baer thought *he can't see me*. But that light was one bright em eff. He stretched himself out on the mushy wet ground to hide his upper body behind a small tree, scanty cover. Foot still in the trap, and stickers on his sleeves, in his hair and pant legs. Rain water still dripping from the trees, he winced in pain and cursed silently. It felt like a medium size trap.

Meanwhile, Rocke had been moving forward slowly, then dropped to the muddy ground when the front door flew open outward. He thought that was strange just as a loud revolver shot whizzed over his head. He returned fire with the silenced AR using three bursts at a time. No need to waste ammo by blowing your whole wad at once.

When Tim heard Jerry open fire he let go of both barrels in rapid succession. He reloaded quickly. John rolled over and let loose with the 30.06, ejecting the rounds as fast as he pulled the bolt and slammed it back. Empty, he dropped the mag and pushed another four rounds in.

"Where is he?" Big John asked.

"What?' Tim fired again.

"Where is he?"

"Can't hear yee. Ears ringing. Just shoot!"

Big John fired again. Jerking the bolt in and out. He didn't know what he was shooting at. Still the four rounds went quickly. '*Tarnation, shoulda brung more ammo.'* One magazine left and he hadn't hit anything but trees. He held his fire.

Baer felt as if his leg had been blown off by the 8 gauge. Splinters flew at his goggles and face. Then larger rounds were coming at him. *Shit.* He lifted and pointed the AR in the direction of the blast and let loose at full auto.

Tim hardly heard Baer's AR16 fire and he dropped the shotgun as bullets hit his hands and torso. He staggered back.

"Jerry, I'm hit. My hands are gone." He started crying. "Jerry! Help me!" Tim fell on his back. "Jerry, I'm hurt bad." No answer from Jerry. "I'm gut shot! Jerry!"

Big John charged out through the back and kept firing where he finally saw Baer's muzzle flashes. "You damn clown!" With all of his shots going wild he luckily managed to hit Baer in the left thigh. Baer saw the flashes and heard the 30-06 firing. He forced himself to sit and shoot left-handed. He pulled the trigger and sprayed the area until empty. He quickly dropped the 30-round mag, slammed in a full one and sprayed the area again, side to side, up and down in a wave. Emptied that and snapped in a new one. But this time he waited, breathing hard with his mouth open. He adjusted the night visions and didn't see anything. *He's either dead or hiding.*

When Rocke fired at Jerry, Jerry never had a chance to return fire. He fell and never got up.

Lil' Pete crawled along the floor, saw Jerry. In anger he shouted, "You out there! Give it up! You're surrounded!"

Rocke lay prone on the muddy ground aiming the AR at the voice. *There's more than two. One down. Three?* "Come and get me, you inbred pervert!"

That pissed Lil' Pete off. He jumped up, silhouetted at the door opening, and fired three quick rounds, wildly, and straight ahead as fast as he could. With one round left in the clip he quickly fed it into the chamber. With his finger on the trigger he yelled, "You dead yet?"

Rocke, lying on the ground, saw the target and hurriedly ejected the mag and shoved in a new one. He let loose with the full mag at full auto. As Pete's body was being jerked around, Murphy's Law kicked in, and his finger twitched and that last round hit Rocke in the right shoulder. Shocked, he knelt up and grabbed his AR with his left hand and continued firing at the body, now on the ground, until empty. No more shots came his way. He cautiously raised himself to a standing position, right arm useless. He slowly approached the door, checked the scene hurriedly and found Jerry dead and the skinny man full of holes. He walked up to Tim with the AR pointed at him. "Jake, hold your fire! I got 'em secured."

"Help me. I'm dying," pleaded Tim, his voice weak now. He lay in his pool of blood.

Rocke looked at him and laid down the AR. With his left hand he wiggled his 915 out and with some difficulty flip the safety down. He pointed the gun between Tim's eyes.

"No! Please!"

Left-handed he squeezed the trigger once. Tim left this world.

Rocke found a dirty cloth on the floor. He grabbed the shotgun with it and tossed it outside into the trees. He took his Tac flashlight off his belt and shined it out. "Jake, where are you?"

"Here." He waved his AR in the air until Rocke's light caught it. "There's an unfriendly out here somewhere but I think I got him. Be careful."

Rocke tucked the small flashlight under his right armpit. He winced with pain. Picking up his AR, he yelled, "I'm coming out." Using his left arm, pointing the AR here and there as he walked slowly through the wet, burr infested, overgrowth. Also mindful of any traps.

Bob Rocke found Big John dead with multiple wounds. Baer was only fifteen feet away. With his AR slung across his shoulders he helped Baer up—after he and Jake got his foot out of the trap. Baer tried to help himself going back to the vehicle, but Rocke did most of the dragging. It took them helping each other awhile to reach Rocke's big Expedition. When they finally reached the Expedition, Rocke put the AR on the front floor. Then he struggled to get Baer up and into the SUV. He gingerly helped Baer into the back seat of the SUV. Rocke's arm was paining and he needed to get a tourniquet on to help stop the bleeding before he fainted from loss of blood. Baer was bleeding too, from his thigh but had on a makeshift tourniquet from a shirt. Being soaking wet made the ordeal worse.

"Next time I'll wear those combat pants with the tourniquets made into the pants. Forgot what they're called, "Baer whispered.

Rocke couldn't tell if Baer was going into shock or delirium.

"Don't know. Be back as quick as I can. Godda clean up a bit."

The only thing he needed to get was Baer's AR. He looked around again with his tac flashlight. He grabbed the AR. He pointed the light to where Baer had been. Clean. Trees and bushes shot to hell, not bad except for Baer's blood stains. Can't help that. Most of it washed away from the rain. The rain started to pick up again.

He walked as quick as he could to get back to Baer. Then he one handed threw the branches willy-nilly, that had covered his Expedition. Using his left hand, he backed out quick and zipped down the road back to the motel. On his way he called the ex-senator on the scrambler which he put on speaker and set it between his legs.

"Speak," Smithe said into the red emergency land-line phone.

"Smithe, we need air e-vac ASAP!"

"Who's down?"

"Jake and myself. He's bleeding pretty bad but I put a tourniquet on his leg, almost stopped. My right shoulder needs a tourniquet. I'll see if a civilian can do it."

A short silence. Then, "How's my son doing?" Smithe was in the Underground with Lewis and Clark for the attack on Gannon's place.

"I think he's stable but he's in pain. If I get a chance, I'll give him some morph. Wish we had blood clotting powder or super glue."

Smithe spoke slowly, "Be careful with the civvies. Hold on." Pushing in the red hold button, he then hit the button on the 1956 six button red Western Electric 564B land line to his spec-ops in Beckley, W.V. He made the call to ex-SEAL Francis Marion, in Beckley, for the extraction of Baer and Rocke.

Smithe got back to Rocke. "Spec-ops has chopper on the way to the motel." Smithe went silent for a few seconds then he spoke quickly. "They'll put down in that business lot across the street. Make sure you're ready. I've told them where to take him. You sanitize the place, pack your ride and drive here."

"To your house?"

"Yes. As fast as you can."

"No can do. I'm shot up bad myself."

"Okay. That's right. I'll send another chopper to get your stuff and sanitize. Hold on." The former senator punched a different button to get former SEAL Richard Hammer and his clandestine team in Martinsburg, W.V.

"Okay, second chopper's on the way," Smithe told Rocke.

"There was a thunder storm earlier so they might run into some weather. It's off and on rain."

"Okay. But they get weather reports, you know," Smithe said.

"That's right. What about Jake's SUV?"

"I'll have someone take care of that. Get ready. They are coming quick." Smithe disconnected. He worried about Baer. He said a prayer for Jake— to make it. Then he pushed a different button to get a former SEAL in Hagerstown, MD. to pick up Baer's SUV.

The helos were coming in from different directions and coming in hot. Flying low at over 140 mph. The vehicles from Hagerstown would arrive much later.

When Rocke arrived at the Inn the proprietor came out. "What's going on?"

"Government business. Is there a doctor or nurse around to help me with my arm? We had an accident."

"Sure. I'll call Doc Willis." He ran inside the B&B.

Curiosity seekers started to gather.

"Back off. Or go to your rooms. Government business!"

Lightning flashed, quickly followed by thunder. Seconds later it poured. The people quickly scattered.

Two minutes later the doctor came speeding up in a Buick, skidded to a stop and jumped out. In his haste he left the wipers on and walked directly to Rocke. "Are you the one hurt?"

"Yes, I need a tourniquet."

Doc Willis had his bag with him. He gave him the once-over. "You need more than that, fella."

Rocke swayed a little. "Just stop the bleeding, I've got help on the way."

"You need…"

"Just do it! And quick."

Doc Willis shook his head. "Let's get out of this rain."

They found shelter under the front porch of the Inn.

"Don't worry. We're government agents. Help's coming." Rocke wiped the rain water from his eyes with his good arm while the doc fixed the torniquet on his other. Then the doc stuffed some gauze into the wound. Rocke winced but made no sound.

After Rocke got patched, he drove the Expedition across the street, parked, left his headlights on and waited. "Come on. Come on." *Thank you, God, for this rain.*

It would wash Baer's blood and keep people away and hopefully confused as to what they saw.

"How're you doing buddy?" Rocke asked.

"Okay. Only hurts if I laugh," Baer said weakly.

"Yeah, me too." Rocke felt a bit woozy. Then he heard, the sputtering sound of the Agusta 109 as it approached. The lightning flashed a couple of times and he saw the flat black bird coming towards them. "You beautiful, Mama."

The first one, Marion's from Beckley, landed and two men raced over to the Expedition. They helped Baer and Rocke into the chopper. As they were put in the chopper, Rocke hoped the other one would arrive soon. The chopper, with its high-pitched whine, revved up and took off with Baer and Rocke both feeling relieved.

Thirteen minutes later, Hammer and the second flat black Agusta 109 chopper from Martinsburg arrived and landed. While the rotors slowed down to idle, three men jumped out wearing sidearms, but not drawn. They raced across the street to the Old Clark Inn. They ran up to Baer's room. The surprised proprietor didn't say a word.

The rain was letting up again.

The three men gathered Baer's and Rocke's belongings and any equipment. Then they sanitized everything in the room.

Hammer saw his men dash out the door and running. One of them detoured. Before the other two reached the copter, the rotors were going full blast. As soon as both men jumped in, with the belongings and equipment, it lifted and sped off. The third man jumped into Rocke's Expedition and drove off, heading north, north east.

Neither helicopter had any identifying markings.

Ten minutes later five troopers arrived, from Troop 3 of the West Virginia State Police, stationed in Marlinton. They were questioning the residents that gathered about. A lieutenant was in charge, ready with his pen and pad. He questioned the proprietor of the B&B. The proprietor informed the lieutenant, "Said they were government agents."

"What government?"

"Danged if I know. Revenuers, maybe."

"How many?"

Everyone said they saw two helpless men and the helicopter people.

"How many from the helicopters?"

Three said six, one said seven, five others said five. The lieutenant shook his head as he wrote all the numbers down. *Bet it was raining.*

"Any numbers on the helos?"

Everyone shook theirs heads or shrugged their shoulders. "Maybe they was Huey's," one of the locals volunteered.

The lieutenant wrote: *Huey's???*

"What kind of vehicle drove off?" the lieutenant continued the questioning.

"A big SUV."

"Color, model."

"Too dark to get the right color and they the hell all look alike," said the proprietor. All agreed with that.

"Tag number."

"Couldn't see. Drove with lights off—in the rain. Damndest thing I ever seen," the proprietor said.

The Lieutenant told his subordinate, "Get crime scene out here, pronto. And tape the parking lot across the street."

He walked back to the small crowd. He asked them, "How many choppers were there?"

This time there was a consensus. They all said two.

Eight minutes later the lieutenant got a call and was told to go see Mr. and Mrs. Klinger. They had heard lots of shooting in the direction of Tim Gannon's place. They told the police no one drove by their house, which was the only way to get to Tim Gannon's place.

"Sergeant, take each witness aside and get their names and exactly what they thought they saw," the lieutenant ordered.

Then the lieutenant and a couple of his men went to Gannon's cabin. The horrific sight slapped them in the face. They had never experienced a slaughter before. Tim was shot multiple times, but the two other persons were chopped meat. Blood spatter was everywhere. A trooper coughed and almost lost his dinner.

The other trooper went to the back of the shack to move away from the carnage and smell. He searched the back, then pointed his 200 lumens flashlight out into the trees. The trooper looked but didn't believe his eyes. He hoarsely said to the lieutenant, "Hey, look at this. No back wall." He cleared his throat. "I bet someone was out in the woods and shot them through the opening."

The lieutenant said, "Both of you go out and look. Check for a nest."

The two troopers went out with their 200 lumens powered flashlights searching. One of the troopers said, "Stop!"

"Whatcha got?"

"Looks like an animal trap." He kicked it with his shoe and it snapped shut. Jumping back, he said, "Damn that was close."

The other trooper felt queasy again. He took in a deep breathe and let it out slowly to calm himself.

Little farther on after passing two other traps they found Big John shot to hell.

Trooper "Queasy" felt sick again. "Aw, shit. Last time I'll go out on a call after just eating."

The other one, George, laughed and said, "Don't like raw meat, huh?"

"Aw, shut up, before I barf on you."

That just made George laugh harder. When he calmed down, he said, "Let's take him back. Fuck the crime scene."

"Shit, George you'll get our asses in trouble."

"Nah. I'll tell 'em it was raining and was washing the DNA anyway. Don't worry, Jim."

They dragged Big John's sorry butt back to the cabin, snapping a trap along the way and had to pry it off of John's ass.

The ambulance finally came and took Tim away first. They knew him.

They had to wait for its return to take the others. While waiting they checked the cabin for clues. George stopped for a second and said, "Let's not wait for the ambulance. Find the keys to that truck outside and put their butts in the bed and haul them to the morgue."

The lieutenant liked the idea so that's what they did.

The lieutenant said, "Jim, call the coroner and tell them that we're taking the bodies to VanReenen's." That was a funeral home in Marlinton.

"Okay." Jim went outside to the patrol car. *Glad to be out of there.*

Later the lieutenant and the other troopers returned from Marlinton and joined the men who were busy at the lot across the street from the Inn. The lieutenant had a limited number of men so he had them process the crime scenes one at a time. When they finished with the parking lot, he would direct everyone to Tim Gannon's cabin.

While they were still at the parking lot, taking pictures, writing notes, and measuring, a man and a woman—unseen, in a Jeep Cherokee, finally arrived from Hagerstown, Maryland. They drove onto the lot of the Old Clark Inn and found Baer's SUV. The woman jumped out and opened the SUV with a special key. She got in, started it and followed the Jeep heading north. Smithe had sent them to pick it up and drive it back to Shady Oaks—before the police found it. Smithe had assets in almost all of the states. When one is a U.S. Senator for a while, you get to know people who know other people who can be an asset.

The only thing the West Virginia State Police or their investigative bureau office could do was gather what messed up evidence they had and bury the dead. The State Police picked up all the 5.56mm NATO brass they could find. No fingerprints on the empties. They knew any other brass came from the decedents. No identifying numbers on the helicopters. No license plate numbers, no color of the large SUV. They didn't see Baer's SUV leave and the proprietor never thought about his mystery guest's vehicle. Their leads were zero. Also, the Florida and Maryland investigators had zip. The only thing the West Virginia State Police knew was that Jerry Gannon was from Takoma Park. Also, that he was a cousin to Tim. No one told them that Jerry was wanted for questioning. The reason being the FBI didn't know where Jerry skipped to. The W.V. State Police never sent out any bulletins; nor did the federal bumbling idiots.

The Maryland and Florida investigators and the FBI investigators finally connected with each other because a diligent lone cold case Baltimore County Police sergeant, Detective Michael Grey, checked all the recent white male deaths in Baltimore County and connected some dots and found out that Jerry Gannon knew Scott Turner from high school. But Jesse Delaney wasn't from their school. None of the dead men had any rape convictions, although one, Jesse Delaney, had two attempted rape charges, but they didn't know where he was. It would be a couple of weeks before anyone discovered Delaney.

They knew about Kenneth Black but he was never tied in with the others. Scott Turner had been arrested for rape but the charge was dropped when the victim changed her story twice. They also didn't know where Turner was. Claudia Turner was on life support—on the COVID-19 floor. If she died, they would count her as a Covid death. If she lived, they would count her as surviving the corona virus.

Elizabeth Crenshaw/Kephart or Abigail Beecher were never contacted about the rapists. Abigail never told anyone but Jake Baer any details, so their names never popped up in the investigations. Abby was still ashamed that she never helped Betty.

27

Baer laid in a hospital bed, in Arlington, Virginia, with his left leg bandaged from his knee to his crouch. His face had some cut marks and bruising. Scratch wounds on arms and hands from burrs and stickers. The night vision goggles saved his eyes. His foot and ankle were also bandaged. He was drugged but coherent when John Smithe walked in.

"I don't pay you to lie around in bed wasting daylight." Smithe smiled.

Grinning Jake said, "Good to see you, too, daddio."

Smithe pulled up a chair and sat close to Baer's head. "Tell me what happened, everything. Later we'll do it right, at the house. I know you're a little woozy."

First thing he said, "The bulletproof vests didn't help us this time."

Smithe told him, "They were crappy shooters."

Jake didn't agree. "They were good enough to hit us."

Smithe grunted.

Then, Baer told him how it went down, as well as he could, being drugged. After he finished, he asked, "What about my leg?"

"They said you should be fine. Took out two double aught balls. They weren't deep. The rest of the shot torn your skin up. Ankle messed up. Going to need skin grafts on both thigh and ankle. Other than that, you should be good as new. You shouldn't have a limp."

"I guess it wasn't time for me to die." He thought that the double aughts had to hit some thickets and brambles and that slowed them down a tad.

Smithe smiled and laid his hand on the leg cast, then said, "No, but it was time for Jerry Gannon and his friends. Bob got him good. Jerry shot at Bob first, then Bob hit him with three bursts automatic fire from his weapon. Then he went after a skinny runt who managed to hit Bob in the shoulder. Took him out. Looked like skinny had more bullet holes in him than Bonnie and Clyde. Bob will be fine though. The bullet didn't hit any major arteries, just capillaries and muscle. I spoke to him before I came here. His room is down the hall. Docs say he won't be able to raise his right arm all the way up."

Baer laughed. "Wanna bet? Good ol' Double R. Always comes through."

Smithe placed his hand on Baer's shoulder. "So do you, son."

"Did they find that other guy?"

"Yes, and he was shot up good, too."

"Good. I did that." He sounded proud. "What about Tim?"

"Died in the house with the others. Bob said he had to finish him off."

Baer smiled and closed his eyes in satisfaction.

"Oh, sweetie. You poor guy." Jane Stafford came rushing through the door. She went to Jake and kissed his lips. He responded in kind.

Surprised by the visit, and before she kissed him again, he had a chance to ask, "How did you know I was here?" She kissed him.

John Smithe said, "Well, I better get going. Get well quick, my boy."

"Come back here you old dog."

Smithe waved on his way out—smiling.

"Don't you blame, John. He called me out of the blue one day asking me all kinds of questions. I said, slow down buddy, who the hell wants to know?" She padded Jake. "Sometimes when I lose my temper, I say some wirty derds." She laughed that laugh he loved. "I'm Lloyd's father, that's who wants to know. And I said, I think he's old enough to make his own decisions. Then he said, he has an important job and I don't want a woman messing his mind up." She laughed again. "Do I mess your mind up…Jake Baer?"

"So, he told you my real name?" He wasn't about to tell her he was thinking of her when he stepped on that damn trap.

"Yes, but I understand you go undercover for Interpol a lot."

"Yes I do. Does that bother you?"

"Does it look like it bothers me? I'm here, right?"

"I'm glad you are. I feel so good I think I'll just get up and go home." He leaned forward.

She pushed him back. "No you don't sweetie. You stay here until you are totally healed." She kissed him on the lips and stayed in that position when she said, "Right?"

With both hands he lifted her head up slightly. "Yes."

She slowly moved away with her eyes closed, smiling.

"What?" he asked.

"Nothing. By the way I have to work tomorrow."

"Flying to Florida?"

"Of course. That's my route for now."

"You mean they can send you…"

"Yep, to San Diego or to Fargo."

"Maybe in the future you can pick your flights—or quit." He grinned a big grin.

"What's that supposed to mean?"

A nurse walked in with a mask on. "Time for your temperature. Oh, company." She looked at Jane. "Are you a relative?"

"Yes, we're kissing cousins," Baer said with a smile.

"Ma'am, I'll have to get you a mask." The nurse started to leave.

"If you don't take my temperature now, I'm getting up and walking out of here. What's more important, my temperature or her wearing a mask?" Baer glared at her hard.

"I guess the mask can wait."

"Forever," Baer replied.

Sighing, the nurse took his temperature, looked at the scan and was about to leave.

"Hold on. What is it?" Baer demanded.

"Ninety-eight point nine." She tried to leave again.

"How about my blood pressure. Maybe you raised it. Take it."

Somewhat flustered, she fumbled the cuff on his arm and started to pump the bulb.

Jane was behind her with her hand to her mouth trying to stifle a laugh. She did a good job. He could be a hard ass with others and she liked that.

The nurse let the air out and took the cuff off.

Baer said, "And?"

"One twenty-five over fifty-one."

"Good girl, you didn't raise it. Off with you now and don't come back."

The nurse glanced at him, went pale and left quickly.

Jane went over to him and kissed him. "You shouldn't be so rough on the hired help." She giggled.

"Honey, please call, John. I'm outta here. I can convalesce at home. And before we leave, I want to see Bob. If he's feeling better, I'll see if he wants to leave."

She got her iPhone and called John Smithe. John came back within fifteen minutes, and had Baer released. After that they went to Double R and had him released. Both were wheeled down to the entrance where Smithe's Ford Explorer SUV was waiting. Jane helped Baer struggle to get in. Rocke slid in easily.

When they were all in, Smithe said, "Let's go Jeeves."

"You made Jeeves a chauffeur?" Baer asked.

"He's certified," Smithe said.

Jake Baer and Bob Rocke had a good laugh.

After the laughter died, Bob looked at Jake, and said, "You look like shit, dog breath."

"So do you, shit for brains."

Jane smiled, shaking her head. She liked that too.

28

Lance Pruitt called Karl Kephart and asked to come over. As Pruitt pulled up to the door Karl walked out to meet him.

Karl said, "Let's take a walk."

Walking across the path and down a trail that meandered through a field, Pruitt started by saying, "It's finished, Karl. All dead plus three extras. No charge for those."

"Extras?"

"Brother of one of the rapists inserted himself into the equation with two buddies. They paid with their lives."

Karl tugged at his ear lobe. "So, it was good."

"Yes. But there are hospital bills. Both of the hirelings got wounded, but will be okay."

"Glad to hear that. They were worth every cent. Send me the bill." He stopped short. "Now I can tell Betty she has nothing to worry about. All of her attackers are dead." Karl smiled and almost chuckled.

"Here's the bill."

"Damn that was quick." He slapped Pruitt on the back.

"Hey, we're up on it. You give me the money and I give it to my contact and he gives to his, and down the line it goes."

"I'd say it was up the line." Karl smacked his right fist into his palm. "Now I have to persuade Betty to go to a Trauma Therapist. I hope all of this will bring my wife back to me."

"I do too," Lance Pruitt said.

"Let's go back to the house," Karl urged.

"Have a seat. I'll be back." Karl left Pruitt on his own. He walked around the room looking at the different branding irons that Karl had hanging on the wall. He admired a large wood structure that hung on the opposite wall with board slats to make a four foot by four-foot wood canvas that had different brands burned into it. Seemed to him Karl was a collector of folk art.

Karl walked in carrying a small canvas bag that said *Return to Federal Reserve*. "Those branding irons are from the eighteen seventies and eighties. Started collecting them when I was eighteen. I burned them into the wood." He dropped the bag on the sofa. It made a jingle sound.

Lance said, "Very interesting and really neat."

Karl got right back to business. "Here's the final payment except for the hospital. Remember to send me the bill."

"I will."

"They'll find ten ounces of gold U.S. American Eagles. The amount we agreed on." Karl stuck out his hand and Lance took it. "Again, they did a great job. Thank them for me."

"I will do that." Lance figured the total price in his head. "Wow, that's over twenty thousand dollars in todays' prices. And that's not counting the extra you already paid."

"Yep. And soon will be worth a lot more."

Lance Pruitt picked up the sack. "It's got some heft to it."

"Be safe and tell them again I said thanks. I can't say that often enough."

"Will do." He left.

That evening Karl sat Elizabeth in a chair with a whiskey sour and he sat close at an angle with his wine.

"Betty, remember that chance meeting we had at Squire's?"

"How could I forget. I thought you were such a handsome brute." She smiled, sipped her drink, her eyes looking over the glass at him.

"Brute? That hurts." He feigned a look of anguish.

"Oh, stop it," she giggled.

"When I saw you, my heart jumped and I had to get to know you. We were so happy—and young."

"Yes, we were…and still are? Right?"

"You know that's right." He poured more wine into his glass and drank some. "I feel young and I want the best for you."

"You've given me the best life I could ever have."

He lifted his glass to her and said," Betty, it's over. You can now really get on with life." He took a sip.

"What are you talking about?"

Whoops wrong choice of words. "Take a swallow."

"That bad." She took a swallow.

"Nope. That good. When you're sleeping, sometimes you moan and say gibberish things. Some words I recognize and know what you are dreaming about. I know subconsciously it's released through your dreams."

"What the heck are you talking about?"

"You know, *the incident* when you were sixteen."

"I don't want to discuss it." She started to rise.

"Please stay. Don't even say anything. You don't have to. Good news. All of them are in Hell now." He took a sip of his wine. "Every last one, gone from this earth." He charged on. "Betty, I would suggest that you get some closure by going to a Trauma Therapist."

"What?"

"Betty, I'm backing you one hundred percent. It would also help me. I'll take you and wait outside during a session. I'll even take some sessions."

"I can't believe you." She started crying. "I don't want to go through that. I don't want to relive it," she sobbed.

He went over to her and knelt and hugged her. "It's for *our* own good. You can stop the sessions any time. You're in control." He started to cry, "Betty, I love you and I want you back." He hugged her tighter.

After a few minutes of them crying she said, "Okay."

29

Baer's house was the first completed in Le Flore County. His house in Shady Oaks sold almost instantly to a house flipper for a nice chunk of change. His new house was slightly larger than the one he had in Virginia. The house had sound deadening rubber floors like the new Underground. The walls were made of state-of-the-art material that repelled eavesdropping of any type—just like the new underground. Plus, plenty of room for military accoutrements of all kinds.

He had the reenforced room he wanted, in the center of his house with access to it from all sides. It would actually be in the middle of the house. The hallway went around it—the safe room. He told his compatriots, think of it like a gazebo with bullet proof walls and steel doors. It was built with as much fireproof or fire-retardant materials as possible.

The house itself would be constructed like a fortress. It would have to be, *if I had kids. What the heck am I thinking?* The doors were steel with wood veneer. The windows were also bulletproof. Brick outside with bullet absorbing materials in between outer and inner walls, with the insulation. Metal roof with the same bullet absorbing sheets underneath. Mortar rounds and larger could get through. Baer thought if that happened, it was the end of the world.

CHAPTER 29

John Smithe's Virginia house was under contract and his house in Oklahoma was breaking ground as Baer was putting the finishing touches on his house. At the same time the new Underground was being dug out. The men doing that work didn't know what the big hole was for. The concrete people would be a different group, as well as different groups for the other parts of the complex. The final work would be done by *Home Restorations* themselves.

Jake Baer and Jane Stafford had been dating as often as they could in the last couple of months. He finally told her what he really did for a living—sort of. He was a problem solver and that made her vulnerable for blowback from his job—if any came.

It upset her somewhat but she changed her home base to Oklahoma City anyway. So what if it was a three-hour drive, she didn't mind the drive, and she loved the state. She also loved the name of the airport. The people were naturally friendly toward her. There's always a couple of bad actors everywhere and one cannot escape from all of the stupid people. Overall, Jake told her, it was a free and safe state.

She also knew that the pay he got for what he did was very good.

After three months of dating Jake had proposed to her and she ecstatically accepted. Their wedding would take place, hopefully, after John Smithe's house was finished. Jake and Jane decided that the wedding would be November seventh, just after the presidential election. Jake was more nervous than if he'd been on a suicide mission. Now he would have to be more careful, more cautious, and less reckless. He would have a wife to think of. He already made one mistake when he stepped on that animal trap.

Another thing Jake worried about the most was that Oklahoma and Texas were getting an influx of people fleeing from other states. Even Kansas reversed the outward trend to an inflow.

The ex-senator worried about it also. He had informed Jake that after the wedding he needed to discuss urgent business with him. Jake pressed him for the details now. No dice. After the wedding.

After the honeymoon, Jane went right to work on putting her touches inside the new house and Jake became a handyman, of sorts, even before the wedding. For Jane, Heavener was a secure place from the world in which she traveled. She thought if they had children, she would "retire". Even by car it didn't take that long to get to some "civilization". She discussed everything when they talked about future plans. Jake was all for it. It made him love her more.

The former senator was anxious for the honeymoon to be over with. He and a few other well to do patriots in business, government and the military were worried about the way the country was heading.

The patriots saw an enemy more insidious than Islam was infecting its way into the fabric of the whole nation. It had started many decades ago and now it seized power through fraudulent means. It was now in their faces. Communism.

30

The trees were almost fully denuded at the end of November in Le Flore County, Oklahoma. This evening Jake and Jane Baer had his mentor, ex-Senator John Smithe, over at their new house near Heavener. Jeeves drove Smithe over even though they were next-door neighbors. It would have been a long walk. Smithe's house had been finished less than a week ago. Took the builders four months—as guaranteed. Also, Baer had healed completely from his ordeal in West Virginia. No limping. Only scars. He wanted those.

"How'd the geeks like their new workplace," Baer asked.

"They love it, they told me today that they found two, one acre lots in Heavener and they're going to build next to each other. Said their wives and kids get along already so living next door won't be a problem, only an asset."

"And I like their wives," Jane said.

"And they like you, my dear," Smithe said and winked at her. She made him feel young.

Chuckling Baer asked, "How does Quark like it."

Smithe said seriously, "He's glad to be back in Oklahoma." Smithe studied Baer's face—then they all laughed.

"As a matter of fact, Quark's come up with a new assignment."

"Quark? Since when does AI give orders for new assignments?"

"Since the Communist party took over the country. Using Covid was a great strategy, using it against the 'unwashed masses.'"

John then asked Baer for names of men he thought would be good for what he had in mind. John Smithe saw the danger and loss of freedom in the country. He thought it was similar to when the British held sway over the colonies. Only this time it was the Communist, not the British. People who don't read or learn from history are doomed to repeat it, he always said. That was where Smithe thought the United States was heading. Another revolution for Liberty. He knew the elections had been fraudulent from his own inside sources.

Baer gave Smithe the names of Robert Rocke, AKA, Bob and Double R, of whom Smithe already knew. Richard O'Shea, AKA, Rick and Ricochet; Francis Marion, AKA, Swamp Fox; Joseph Sledge; and Richard Hammer. All were former Navy Seals. They all lived in different parts of the country and were well insulated. They would all be NOCs, pronounced Knock, which means they will have—no official cover, only being attached to themselves and each other. John Smithe knew and used a couple of them in Jake's last assignment with the rapists. The ex-senator would provide any cover for them—if he could.

Smithe also had other people he knew and could use. Former Rangers, Green Berets and Night Hawks.

"What's the assignment?" Baer didn't like where this was going, but he was a patriot.

"You will team up with, of course, the geeks and Quark. Plus, their brothers, Holmes and Watson, in the NSA, are on standby. They are already working on the preliminary plans. Operation code name—*Bunker Hill.*"

Jane Baer put her hand up to her mouth. She remembered from her high school history class that in 1775, the Sons of Liberty first battled the British on Bunker hill in the war for independence, and that the Patriots won on a technicality, as people would say today. That was good, but she didn't want to be a widow. It would not be a good time to die.

Acknowledgments

Again, my thanks to M.Sgt. Gary Knight of the Oklahoma City Police for his help whenever I needed it. Also, to Jane Hirsch for giving me some great ideas and catching pesky mistakes. Thank you again Eric Lueb for your fine tune editing. You caught some clumsy writing that needed re-writing. All of you made this a better fiction novel.